THUS BEGAN THE WAR IN HEAVEN—

"They heard it then. The three clear notes had come to me first and, the second time, they seemed to cut through the heavy air with vibrating urgency. The notes were long drawn, filled with warning and alarm. Echoing long after, the breath that blew them was still. They sounded an end to all that I had known and I was suddenly afraid.

"Then the enemy was upon us—clothed in black, silver serpents blazoned on their tunics —as though the trees had drawn back to reveal rank on rank of dark horsemen.

"I saw now that the horizon was on fire, and heard from the heavens a great roaring—a battling, raging hurricane, trampling the air like stampeding horses. . . ."

CHAMIEL was ~~originally~~ published by Quartet Books Limited.

CHAMIEL

by

Edward Pearson

PUBLISHED BY POCKET BOOKS NEW YORK

CHAMIEL

Quartet edition published 1973

POCKET BOOK edition published November, 1974

This POCKET BOOK edition includes every word contained
in the original, higher-priced edition. It is printed from
brand-new plates made from completely reset, clear, easy-to-
read type. POCKET BOOK editions are published by POCKET
BOOKS, a division of Simon & Schuster, Inc., 630 Fifth
Avenue, New York, N.Y. 10020. Trademarks registered
in the United States and other countries.

To John

CONTENTS

PART ONE

"You haven't been here for a long time."

"I've had other visits to make."

"Why?"

"One of my brothers was sent on a journey beyond the earth and I said I would do his visits for him, while he was away."

"Why did he have to go on a journey?"

"Michael sent him with a message."

David sat up in his bed and stared at the man with brown eyes and long brown hair who was leaning over the bed rail and smiling.

"D'you know what the message was?"

"No. But it was to the Black Angel."

"In Hell?"

"Yes."

The little boy looked through the open window at the starlit sky.

"Did he get back all right?"

"Of course."

After some thought, David asked,

"You said, once, that the stars were holes in the floor of Heaven through which the Angels peep, didn't you?"

"Yes. That was on account of something which the Black Angel did a long time ago."

"I remember. But you never told me why. Will you?"

Chamiel came and sat on the bed nearer the child.

'It was a terrible time,' he said. 'Although I was there, I couldn't remember everything that happened. The broth-

11

ers have told me things since then which I had forgotten.

I was at Michael's Court in those days. There were about ten of us younger ones. We had been sent there for training in History, Rights and Behavior, and were divided into pairs for instruction from Michael himself or Gothric or from one of his lieutenants. Sometimes Gabriel himself would teach us, but not often. I was paired with Abdiel who was the oldest and most experienced among us. I was the youngest.

One morning, Abdiel and I were on yard duty in the forecourt. We were playing a game of checks in the sand. I remember how annoyed Abdiel got because the tree shadows crept over the lines we had drawn and they were hard to see. Suddenly we heard the sound of horse's hooves thudding on the grass outside the Court, and, before either of us could stand up, a horseman galloped into the yard. For a moment we were spellbound. I had never seen such a sight. When the dust had settled, there stood a proud, black stallion whose coat shone like polished ebony and whose thick tail flicked impatiently from side to side. But when I looked at the rider, I drew my breath in with a hiss. I saw that Abdiel was staring at him wide-eyed, too. The rider was tall and slim and the sun shone off his long, golden hair. His face was brown and handsome with a narrow, straight nose and a mouth which seemed always to be smiling. His eyes sparkled like cold sapphires. He wore a black, pleated tunic which came down to his thighs and his legs were tightly sheathed in black leather. Short, scarlet leather boots came up to his ankles and there was a device of silver serpents worked on the boots. Around his waist was a wide, silver belt and from it hung, on a fine silver chain, a black leather pouch and the clasp of the pouch was a snake's head.

Remembering our duty, we ran forward to the stranger. I went to the horse's head and lightly took the reins. I

12

noticed that the martingale was embossed with silver eagles and that the steel curb chain was fashioned of entwined serpents. Abdiel stood ready to answer the rider's questions. He smiled at us and chuckling, said:

"Playing games instead of doing duty?" His voice was deep and soft.

Abdiel blushed and I moved so that my face was hidden by the horse's head.

"Is Michael here?"

"Yes. In the Court," Abdiel answered.

"Take my horse into the shade. Don't feed or water him. I shall not be long—I think."

He dismounted and, tucking a pair of red gauntlets into his belt, walked with light strides to the stone steps. He went up them three at a time and disappeared with a sudden laugh under the cool portal.

Abdiel and I were silent as though the stranger's presence had forbidden us to talk about him. I looped the reins through a ring in one of the chestnut trees and loosened the stallion's girths. Then I sat at the foot of the tree tearing green leaves into idle patterns. Abdiel walked about. There was a frown on his forehead and he shook his black hair. I said:

"What's the matter?"

"He's a swashbuckler——" he answered and came and stood over me. I looked up and saw that his black eyes were troubled.

"Didn't you see——" but before Abdiel could say any more, we heard the drone of voices from the Court and again heard the stranger's laugh. I sprang to the horse and by the time that I had led him to the middle of the forecourt Michael, Gabriel and the stranger had reached the bottom of the steps. I saw the stranger turn to Gabriel. He seemed to ask a question. Gabriel shook his head and his white beard swung from side to side as he answered fiercely, waving a finger when he spoke. The stranger shrugged his shoulders and turned towards us. He

13

was smiling. I brought the horse to him and Abdiel helped him to mount. For a moment he sat with the reins looped over his forearm, drawing on his gauntlets. Then he leaned down and said,

"Thank you, Abdiel and Chamiel," and winked as though he shared some secret with us. He turned his horse, raised an arm in salute to Gabriel and Michael and was gone."

Chamiel was silent then, until David asked,
"Who was he?"

'I'll tell you, if you're patient. I remember that after he had left the forecourt we all stood exactly where we were. Quite still. And the brightness had gone from the day. Michael called me and Abdiel went to Gabriel. I walked on Michael's right side and Abdiel was on Gabriel's right side and we passed slowly out through the South Gate into the gardens. We walked beneath the holm oaks and eucalyptus trees and it was cool. Michael and Gabriel talked together in low voices and solemnly. I tried to understand their words and heard Gabriel say:

"I must go to the Great Court now and ask for guidance."

After a while, I did not listen any more and I thought about the stranger and his horse. But I could not keep my mind on them. I knew that Michael was vexed. I knew that because when he put his hand on my shoulder, I felt how taut it was and, once, after Gabriel had said something to him, he clenched his fingers so suddenly that I put my hand onto his hand. He looked down on me then and I saw in his gray eyes that he had forgotten about me. He smiled and patted my shoulder but I knew that he was not thinking about me.

Before I went to sleep that night, I asked Abdiel:
"Who was he?"
"Who?"

14

"You know—the rider who came today."

"Zareal—Prince of the Southern Palatine."

"What did he want?"

"I don't know. Go to sleep."

But I think he knew. However, I did not say any more then.

After Zareal's visit, things changed and our quiet life became forgotten. Nobody seemed to have the time for answering questions or for doing the things which they did before. Michael was gentle and patient but, whenever I spoke to him, his mind seemed to be elsewhere. Noral, the Trumpeter, was forever coming and going. His bony body and long, swinging arms would be seen moving urgently across the yard, or about the Court, or in the stables at all times of the day and night. Often he would be away for days at a time. When he returned, his face was always thinner and grayer than before.

One morning when Abdiel and I were copying out some of Gabriel's revelations and we were alone in the Little Hall, I said:

"Abdiel?"

"Yes?"

"What's all this commotion about, these days?"

He did not answer at once but leaned against his teak desk and kept smoothing his hair with the palm of his hand. At last he came over to me, very serious, and said:

"Chamiel—it's war."

"War?"

"Yes. War."

"There can't be a war here!"

"You'll see. Zareal came that day in the hope of persuading Michael to side with him against—against," Abdiel hesitated and then went on with a rush of words, "against the Lord and the Great Court."

"The Lord?" I broke in. "Zareal must be mad."

"No. He's wrong but not mad," Abdiel went on. "I

talked to Gothric about it. Michael sent for Gothric when Zareal had gone. Gothric said that Michael and Gabriel told Zareal that he hadn't a chance of taking over the Kingdom. Gothric had been hearing rumors about Zareal's doings for some time but he hadn't believed them. After he'd been to the Great Court, Gabriel went to see Zareal and spent two days with him, trying to stop him going on with his scheme. Gothric heard Gabriel tell Michael that Zareal's arguments for a revolt seemed so strong that Gabriel wondered at times who was wrong and who was right. In the end he came away having done nothing. Zareal just laughed when Gabriel told him he'd been thrown out forever."

"But he doesn't stand a chance. So why's everyone so bothered?" I asked.

"You're wrong. Zareal has great power and he's been making preparations for a long time. Gothric says all the South will come with him and possibly some from the northern March and around Zara, where all the new entrants are. It'll be chancy."

We were silent until Abdiel said:

"Now you see why there's been so little laughter here lately."

I answered, "Yes."

In the following days, everyone was grim and quiet. We younger ones kept out of the way when there was no duty. We did not shout or sing or have the wild games outside the Court——"

Chamiel stopped speaking. He stared through the open window and was still for so long that David asked:

"What's the matter? What happened after that?"

Chamiel turned, and when he moved the crystal circle which hung from a gold chain around his neck caught the light and burst into a blaze of rainbow colors. He laid his hand on David's and went on.

'I was thinking of the next happening. In itself it was not very important. Yet I remember it so well because it marked and ended a certain period for me, and because it brought me something which I had never had before—fear.

Yes, I was afraid. I will tell you why. It was the time of day when we rested. I was lying on the grass outside the Court with Abdiel and two of the other young ones. The air was heavy—not hot—but burdened. There was no wind, not even a sigh. The leaves of the aspens by the Gateway hung still and unwinking. We did not talk, as was our habit at that hour.

Suddenly I sat up, saying, "Listen."

Abdiel and the others moved lazily and looked at me.

"What?" asked Abdiel.

But I did not answer. I was standing up, straining my whole body to catch the sounds again.

"There—the bugle——" I almost shouted.

They heard it then. The three clear notes had come to me first and, the second time, they seemed to cut through the heavy air with vibrating urgency. The notes were long drawn, filled with warning and alarm. Echoing long after the breath that blew them was still. They sounded an end to all that I had known and I was suddenly afraid.

At the third call, they were louder and all within and about the Court heard them. The forecourt filled with brothers, some of whom ran outside the walls. They were anxious and questioning. Some strained their eyes in the direction from which the bugle call had come. Then, down by Heli woods, at the entrance to one of the rides, I saw Noral. I saw him rein in his mare, raise his bugle and sound once more the three dreadful notes. I heard them fade away into the woods, but before the last echo had gone, Noral was but a stone's throw from us all, waiting, silent and wondering. The crowd pressed back to give him

17

way. Hands were lifted in salute, but no one questioned him.

As he passed me, I saw that his face was flushed and that his forehead was white with salt-dried sweat. He rode straight to the steps, dismounting while his mare was still moving and before Abdiel could reach him. He disappeared into the Court and, as soon as he was out of sight, a sudden burst of talk exploded among us. I pushed my way to Abdiel and stood beside him, trying to catch his eye. At last, knowing what I wanted, he said:

"This is war."

My mind was so full of questions that I said nothing but wondered what I should have to do if it was war.

Then Michael came out to the top of the steps with Gothric at his side. When I looked at them standing there, I realized how strong and powerful Michael was. He was tall, even taller than lanky Noral. His hair was short and gray and curled. His eyes were gray and when he laughed and, sometimes when he was angry, he would open them very wide. He was broad and powerful and his presence spoke of great strength, calmness and great confidence.

We were all silent, our eyes fixed on him. He put one hand on the golden circle worked on his white blouse and then spoke.

"My brothers," he said, "Noral has brought news which many of us expected, all of us feared. Zareal has raised the Southern Palatine and marches against the Lord. Odach from the North is moving to join him and many of the Borderlanders are already at his side. He has scourged and laid waste the lands to the north of the Principality and heads with all speed for the Great Court." Michael paused and at once there rose awed murmurs from his listeners. He held up his hand for silence.

"Time is short and we shall leave at once. Gothric and his lieutenants have their orders which will be passed to you. We shall march to cut off the Black Angel, as he must now be called, and his hordes. At Lilla we shall be joined by the levies of Brigit and Og. We are, even with these, outnumbered by the forces of evil who will use every wicked device to overcome us. But——" Michael paused again, "we have faith—faith that the Lord's might will drive back Zareal and all his sinful arms. We shall throw them to utter destruction. By faith and courage we shall prevail. We shall prevail."

He ended and at these words a loud and happy shout broke from the throng and Michael smiled. From that moment the care and doubt, which had drugged us all, vanished. We were renewed by excitement, energy and determination.

Gothric called to the lieutenants and, after a few words with them, they issued orders to the brothers who then quickly dispersed and went about their duties. Gothric, seeing that I was alone, beckoned to me and——"

"Chamiel?"
　"Yes?"
　"What was Gothric like?"

'He was not tall—not with the great stature of Michael. He was square. His tunics were almost sleeveless and showed his arms springing like cordwood from his bull-like shoulders. His chest was a mountain of muscle and he carried himself with dignity. His short, thick legs were black-haired like the backs of his hands. I used to watch the muscles swelling and stretching in his legs when he walked and sometimes I wondered why they did not burst through the skin. His nose had been flattened and his face was always pale making his eyes remarkable. They were large, shining and bronze-colored, like those of the falcon. Often, when I was beside him, and he moved his hands, I would see the wide silver bangle around his right wrist stretch against the strain of the muscles of his forearm.

19

It was a thing soon passed from mouth to mouth that Gothric was a great captain. We never doubted it. To us he was always the same, quiet, and kindly spoken—like one who having a great strength has learned how little it need be used.

When he beckoned to me, I went to him.

"We haven't forgotten you, Chamiel," he said. Below his long, black moustache, his lips lifted into a wide smile. "You report to Michael's houseman."

"Where's Abdiel?" I asked.

"He'll be with me and you'll be with Michael."

"Michael? Me?" I said, in amazement.

"Yes. Someone must think a lot of you. Now then, double up. We haven't got all day. We march in an hour."

I ran into the bustling Court and up the wide marble stairs through Michael's anteroom, empty now, and to his private chamber where I found the white-haired houseman.

"I've come, Xene," I said.

"High time, too," he answered.

"Gothric's only just told me I had to."

"Don't chatter, boy. Follow me."

I went with him into Michael's sleeping room.

"Undress," said Xene and brought me a white tunic with a short, pleated skirt which I put on. The blouse of the tunic was decorated with a red circle on the chest. Xene gave me a gold belt to put around my waist and for my feet a pair of thickly soled sandals of red leather. There were gold buckles on the sandals. He then took me to a table at one side of the room and said:

"These are yours," and pointed to the things which were on the table top. He first took up a white sheepskin coat and dropped it back again. Then a short staff made of polished boxwood and, lastly, a small black leather pouch, worn and creased and closed by a leather strap. Xene took this and fixed it to my belt, asking:

20

"You know what these things are for?"

"Yes," I replied, "except this," and I touched the pouch.

"I'll tell you about that later," he said. "Come over here."

He went to a black basket, placed in the middle of the room. The lined lid was open.

"In this is all that Michael will need while he is away. At the bottom are two blankets. The red one is yours, the white one is his. It is your duty to look after these things. To see that they are at hand when he wants them. This box will be in the first wagon of the baggage train. You will see that it is brought to his tent whenever the tents are pitched. More important than these duties, is the duty you will have in taking every possible care from Michael's shoulders. He has a load to bear and heavy responsibilities. You must lighten them as far as you can. You will go by his side and serve him in all ways. Let him have nothing more than his own great task to think of."

To all this I nodded and said "Yes."

"Now," went on Xene, as he took a small book from the top of the basket. The book's covers were of polished horn and the pages fastened with a copper lock. "This is Michael's book. In it are the teachings of the Lord. Each night, at whatever time he goes to his rest, you will read to him from this book. You will find that I have marked the readings which he prefers or which I think right. You will do this every night, whether he forbids you to or not. You will read to him whatever he says. Do you understand?"

"Yes."

"Even if he should lose his temper, you will continue to read."

"Yes."

Xene then put the book and its key into the pouch.

"That is all. Take up your own belongings. I will see that Michael's are put into the wagon. Go to the stables and take Michael's horse to the main gate and wait for him there."

As I moved across the room, I looked out into the forecourt. It was crowded now and many brothers had fallen into their ranks. I hurried, catching up the coat and staff and running to the doorway. But Xene called:

"Chamiel."

I stopped and turned back to him.

"You will forget yourself," he said, "you will serve Michael and remain strong and courageous."

"I will."

"The Lord will keep you." '

Chamiel paused in his story and then went on.

'So we left Michael's Court. He rode at the head of the long column. I walked beside him with the staff in my hand. We passed through the heavy scented woods and came down onto the wide plain where the cattle feed. Here, my feet shook the pollen from the flowering grasses and clouds of wax-white moths fluttered up into the air. In the distance, I saw the gray outline of the Noon Mountains to which we were making our way. Lake Vassey was a silver medallion in the dark green plain when we came to it and there Michael halted us. I waited to see if he wanted anything of me and then ran back through the groups of singing, chattering brothers to find Abdiel. But we were called to the march before I had time to look far. When we moved from the lake, four swans rose from the waters and flew with us till dusk. I watched them turn away then in a wide circle over Michael and fly back down the marching columns. As they went, hands and faces were lifted in greeting to them. Later, I looked back to see the four dark specks fading into the evening light. By dark we had entered one of the valleys among the foothills, where we halted. Michael told me to fetch Gothric to him, which I did and they conferred. The lantern I had lighted and set at their feet threw such shadows on their faces that I would not have recognized Michael but for the beauty of his eyes, nor Gothric save for the fierceness of his moustache.

Michael said,

"We can stay here but two hours. I have thought that because Zareal can move fast—faster than we can—he will make for the mountains at Blendinah and for the Kopal Pass. That is his quickest way. Our only chance to cut him off is to reach the pass first and to stand between him and it. Therefore, we cannot go to Lilla to meet Brigit and Og. You must send Noral and two others and they will lead them to us through the Kopal."

I saw Gothric shaking his head and then pull his moustache with horny fingers. He said:

"With this small force, you can't hold back Zareal and all his hordes."

"We can. In that narrow place it will not need many to hold back many."

Gothric shook his head again but Michael went on:

"We will. Though Noral must use all speed and so must we."

"Noral shall go at once."

When Gothric had gone, Michael sat down.

"Chamiel—lie down and sleep, for there will be little sleep for us all from now on."

"And you, Michael?" I asked.

"I will rest," he answered.

He sat with his back against a boulder and I brought him my sheepskin coat for a pillow. But he shook his head. So I spread it on the ground at his feet and sat on it. I undid the pouch and took out the book. By the lantern's soft light I read to him and when I had finished the reading, he smiled and patting my hair, said:

"Thank you, boy. Now sleep a little and I will wake you."

But I stayed awake and when I heard the shouted

orders and the sudden stirring below and saw the moving lights, I fetched Michael's horse, and from then till daylight I led it. In front of me went our guide, carrying a lantern. I, too, carried a lantern slung on the boxwood staff.

Nobody talked as we slowly climbed higher and higher. The only sounds were those of the scuffing horses' hooves, the shuffling of many feet or the sudden squeal from a dragged wagon wheel. Occasionally we passed a goat, its eyes like agates in the flickering light and, once, the whiteness of an owl floated over us, its wings spread wide, and slowly vanished into the darkness.

At dawn we halted again. This time fires were lighted and we took food and drink. I brought Michael his and asked:

"Where are we?"

"On the Noon Mountains, near the top ridges. We shall follow along this side and by midday we shall be at Blendinah and the Kopal."

When he had finished his food, he got up from the rock on which he had been sitting and said:

"Come with me."

It was fully light. The fires sent twisting pillars of smoke into the morning air which smelled sweetly of burning sapodilla wood. Michael led me away from the track which we had followed all the night and we climbed straight up the mountainside until we reached an outcrop of red rocks. Michael scaled these, stopping at times to give me his hand. On the top I found that I was standing on a flat shelf of stone which jutted out from the mountain. Below was the valley through which we had come during the night. Mist now clouded it and stretched from its mouth in a gray veil across the foothills and beyond to the plain.

"That is the way we have to go," Michael said, pointing to the right. I turned and looked along the mountain

24

range. The dark peaks rose out of the mists like the backs of breaking waves.

"But this is what I have brought you to see," he went on. "There."

Where the last of the hills ended, the forest lands stretched in black ribbons and beyond them the country rose and fell with gentle hills and valleys and these were patched and shaded with every kind of green. In the middle of this country one large, rounded hill rose above all the rest. It lay between us and the rising sun and from its wide base to its flattened crown this hill was circled with mounting rows of buildings, whose towers, spires and domes rose up like jeweled fingers. At the top, crowning them, was a shining Court, set like the brightest, largest stone in a beautiful ring. The air above this city shimmered with a thousand twinkling lights as dew on a spring morning."

"Just like your circle did, when you moved," David said.

"Yes. Just like that," Chamiel answered. "I remember that I stood so long looking at it that Michael laughed and took me by the sleeve and said:

"Come along. We must return. You and I will go to that City when this is over."

At midday, as Michael had said, we reached Blendinah and there we halted some little way below the Kopal. Michael sent me for Gothric. I found him with his lieutenants and Abdiel was with him. Abdiel and I smiled at each other but did not speak. I think that because we were now so near the enemy, I was too excited to speak. The three of us joined Michael at the head of the column. When he saw Abdiel he laughed, saying:

"You look as though you have had a dust bath."

Abdiel answered, smiling, "I feel like it. It's clean for Chamiel marching in front. But halfway down and right under Gothric's horse you can't see anything for dust and stones."

Michael turned to Gothric with the words:

"We will reconnoiter," and nodded in the direction of the pass.

Abdiel asked if he and I were to come, and Michael gave permission, adding:

"There will be a wind through the Kopal. There always is. It will blow some of the dust off you. But remember, both of you, on no account are you to show yourselves on the skyline. For all we know, Zareal may be halfway up the other side."

We climbed in silence and before we reached the pass Gothric signed for us to stop. He spoke in a low voice.

"You two can go through first. One on each side of the pass. You will not talk and you will conceal yourselves as much as you can. Crawl, if necessary. When you reach a place from which you can see everything on the other side, you will look for the Black Angel's armies. When you see them, come back and report to me here. I shall want to know where they are and how far they are from the pass. If you don't come back in a reasonable time, we shall bring all the forces into the mouth of the pass. Understand?"

Abdiel said "Yes" and I nodded.

As I moved away, Gothric called softly:

"Hi, Chamiel, you don't need that magician's wand. Leave it with me."

I did so, slowly.

I took the shaded side of the pass. It was as cold as a mountain stream and the wind pulled at my hair and brought tears to my eyes. My heart was beating heavily and I could hear it drumming in my ears. I moved stealthily from boulder to boulder and glanced every now and then towards Abdiel. He was well ahead of me and I had difficulty in seeing him. The sides of the pass widened at the far end and the way through became broader with no boulders but only loose stones. When I saw the far skyline and I knew that I was on the other side, I crouched down and ran till I had caught up with Abdiel. I lay beside him without a word.

D'you remember how I said that the north side of those mountains was like the back of a rolling wave? The side on which we now were was like the front of that wave. The peaks and crests leaned over as though they would fall and break on the earth below and the shadows of the mountains stretched out into the Southern Plain like wolves' teeth. Beneath us, the track wound through a short gorge and finally came out onto the lowland. At this point was a small hill set like a sentry to guard the track to the pass.

Abdiel touched my sleeve and said:

"No sign of them. Though it's difficult to see in all this haze. I've seen this land before and on a clear day you can see across the plains and downs to the edges."

I did not answer because I was looking at every detail of the country below. Then, out on the plain I saw a dark gray mass. It might have been a wood or dark earth or bog, but I knew what it was. And as soon as I knew it, I wanted to run away. I trembled a little and could not take my eyes off the enemy. I was on my stomach, my hands tucked below my chest, and I said:

"There they are."

I dared not take my hand from below my body and point for fear that it would tremble.

"Where?" asked Abdiel.

"Wait till the haze moves. Now. You see what looks like a river? You see the bend?"

"Yes."

"To the right of that."

He stared and then said:

"It's not. It's just marsh or something."

"It isn't. It's Zareal."

"How d'you know?"

"Because I just know. That's why. I know it is."

Abdiel looked at me without saying anything and then turned again to stare at the dark mass.

"I believe you're right. Every now and then you get a sudden sparkle as if the sun was reflected off something bright."

He got up.

"I'm going back."

"They're about four hours from here," I said.

"Right. You coming?"

"No. I'll stay."

"You'd better come."

I remembered my duty to Michael and went with Abdiel. From that moment I felt that I was no longer myself. I went about in a state of wonder and it was not until after the fearful happening of that night that I came to myself.

Abdiel reported the enemy's position and then events moved quickly. The wagons and draft horses were left on the north of the pass, while Michael led his men through it to the bottom of the track and under the lee of the hill. He gave orders for a rest but forbade the lighting of fires and singing. In a little while Gothric came to him and they discussed battle positions. I was clearing away the remains of a meal and when I came back I sat behind them. Michael was saying:

"Noral will not reach Lilla before tonight. Brigit and Og will march through the night, but cannot reach us much before tomorrow in the late afternoon. We must hold on here until they arrive."

Gothric agreed and added:

"I shall divide our force into three. The first group will take up a position across the track, just short of the hill. There," he pointed. "Behind them, I'm putting the second and stronger section, also astride the track where it levels out." He turned and pointed again, to a place where the track narrowed and where, on one side, it was bounded

28

by walls of sheer rock. "The third section will be reserves and out of sight in the gorge, higher up. The first group, with you, will bear and blunt Zareal's attack for as long as possible and can then fall back on the second position. I know that there's always the risk that Zareal will try a flanking move and pin us against those rocks, but we shall have to accept that. His force is mostly cavalry, so I think he'll rely on his numbers and speed to break through quickly and frontally. Do you agree?"

"Yes. I agree about the risk to our flanks, but we shall have to accept that and you must hold the reserves against such an event. Where are the observers?"

"There's a post at the top of the hill."

"Good," Michael answered. "Now, I expect him to reach us at dusk. So there'll be no fighting tonight. Once they know that we are here, you can let the brothers light fires. But get them into position well before dawn tomorrow and see that all know exactly what is expected of them. There must be no confusion. You can stress the advantage that our position needs few men to hold it. And held it must be."

"Very well."

"Go and see to these things and then get some rest and the Lord be with you."

After Gothric had gone, Michael paced up and down in thought, sometimes stopping to look across the plains. At last he said:

"Chamiel, I am going to the hilltop—to have a look at Zareal."

I got up and picked up my staff.

"There is no need for you to come," he said.

"But I will. I have good eyes," I replied.

He laughed and added, "and as good a heart."

We left the track and followed a sheep road up the hill. The air was scented by thyme and gorse flowers and the grass bright with orchids and weeds. But I only remembered these things afterwards, for at that time there

29

was a throbbing anxiety inside me. Halfway up the hill Michael stopped, looked back and began to speak.

"You are anxious. So am I. For now is the time of trial. In action fear is lost, anxiety gone. Now is the time to pray that the Lord will leave your mind clear, your decisions quick and your actions right. There will be little time soon to do more than fight for Him. So you see that I know what you are feeling. You quake. You fear the unknown. But ask for courage and you will get it."

He put his hand on my shoulder and asked:

"I am right?"

"Yes."

"Remember one thing above all—the Lord will prevail. That is certain. He will not allow us to be routed. Yet for all that, it cannot but be a bitter fight and when you feel that there is no hope, remember that the Lord will triumph. Will you believe that?"

"I do," I answered.

"Good. Let us go up."

We found the watch post manned by one brother in the shelter of a small rabbit warren.

"Every now and then," the brother said, "you can see them, or rather you can feel where they are."

He pointed across the strip of scrubland which stretched away from the foot of the hill towards a thick belt of elm, oak and sycamore trees.

We watched in silence. Only our eyes moved. When I saw the rooks rise in noisy fear above the trees and the pigeons fly towards us at speed, I touched Michael and pointed to the woods. But what came from the woods was not our enemy. It was animals—foxes, badgers, rabbits, ermine, weasels, flying as though from a forest fire. Once out of the woods they scattered in all directions and became invisible. For a while there was no movement save for the bobbing rooks. Then the enemy was there—as though the trees themselves had drawn back to reveal rank on rank of dark horsemen—silent and hazed in steam. There was no color in all their numbers. As I stared, with my mouth open and drawing in my breath as quietly as I could, two riders joined them. In the failing light we watched them trot to the leader, pause there for a moment and then ride around the ranks and disappear into the trees.

"They've seen us," the brother whispered.

"We will go back," Michael answered.

We hurried to our camp and Michael gave the news to Gothric, who immediately put his men into battle positions. Then he and Michael made a tour of the lines and I was left to put the tent in order. When I had done this, I went up to Gothric's tent and found Abdiel. We sat outside and talked in the gloom until Gothric's return. I found Michael in his tent. He was writing by the lantern's light. I said nothing but went to my blanket which was spread at the foot of the tent. It was dark now and the camp noises had died to muffled murmurs. Michael stopped writing and laid the written sheets away in a small wooden box. After he had lain down, I waited, hearing the sentry's heavy tread outside. Then I took the book from my pouch and squatting near Michael, where the light fell on the yellowed pages, I started to read to him. At the sound of my voice, he said:

"Not tonight. I have much to think of."

I went on reading softly.

"Did you hear what I said? I do not wish to be disturbed."

I took no notice. But I could not prevent my voice from quavering. Michael raised himself on his elbow. I kept my eyes on my book.

"Chamiel, obey me at once. Stop reading."

I shut the angry tones from my mind. I drowned his voice with the words which I was reading.

"Chamiel, if you do not stop, I shall call the guard and have you sent back to the baggage."

But I kept on and suddenly I heard a long sigh and,

looking up, saw that he was lying with his eyes closed. I thought that he slept but when I had finished and I rose and stood beside him, he smiled and lifting his hand said:

"Forgive me, Chamiel."

I went to my blanket but did not sleep. I lay listening to Michael's breathing and the regular movements of the sentry and then I crept from the tent. I told the sentry that I was too hot in the tent and that I was going to get cool and would walk about for a while. I picked my way through the lines and came to the foot of the hill. I saw that the sky behind the hill was colored by red flickering.

"They have lighted the fires," I said to myself. This light grew brighter and began to stretch higher and higher across the sky until I had to bend my head backwards to see its margin. From the top of the hill I saw that the horizon was on fire. At intervals in the line of flame, there were great burning jets which threw their pronged tongues in wide licks against the night. I watched them with amazement. I heard the excited noises from Zareal's camp and saw the jiggling of many lanterns. The enemy voices came to me like the croaking of bullfrogs. Suddenly, from the middle of each jet of flame a narrow, fiery cone sprang upward, trailing a fan of white sparks. I could hear the crackling hiss of their flight. Then, as though all of them were guided by one hand, they changed their upward flight and flew on a course towards the mountains and our camp. At this, I turned and ran down the hill. When I reached the sentry and before he could say anything to me, I told him to wake Gothric and to bring him to Michael's tent. I shook Michael awake, saying:

"Quick. Come and see. I've sent for Gothric."

We stood outside and I pointed, needlessly, to the sky. Michael looked at the thousands of flying cones and muttered:

32

"Devil's work."

The bugle blew and was followed by sudden noises and clamor. Gothric came to Michael.

"They're all at battle stations," he said. Michael, watching the sky, answered:

"If these fall on us, as Zareal intends, we shall be doomed and his work will be crowned."

The long cones flew gradually lower and lower and the whine of their flight was clearly heard, echoing from the sky above. Our camp was silent but below the hill there were cheers.

I looked at Michael. He was standing with his head thrown back, taut, and his hands clasped across the circle on his chest. His lips moved and in that strange light from above I saw sweat standing in little pearls on his forehead. Gothric was silent. I moved closer to Michael, one hand gripping my staff tightly. Abdiel came and stood beside me and I put my other hand into his.

Then, above the whirring of the cones, I heard a whisper—little more than a sigh. It came from behind us, from behind the high mountains. The whisper became a whistling, high pitched and soon screaming like the wind through ships' rigging. Then the whistling was a great roaring and from up and over the mountain tops there swept down the sky a battling, raging hurricane, trampling the air like stampeding horses. We felt it sweep over us and leave us breathless. We saw it hit the cones and lift them, with an angry hiss, up and away from us, scattering them in all directions but ours. They were hurled away from us like feathers. We watched them slowly fall to earth and, as each one fell, it burst with a white flash at which both the air and the ground shuddered. On every side we saw these flashes and felt the thuds as they dug themselves into the ground.

And when they saw this and knew that they had been saved, a triumphant cry went up from Michael's men. But there was silence below the hill.

33

"The Lord has saved us," Michael said. We did not speak. Gothric was breathing heavily and I felt Abdiel's hand clenching and unclenching around mine. At last Gothric went to stand the men down and Michael moved slowly to his tent. I asked Abdiel:

"What were they?"

"We shall never know. Some work of the Black Angel."

Before the first light, the bugle sounded again. I went with Michael, Gothric and Abdiel to inspect the brothers. Michael knew each one by name and had encouragement for all. His assurance heartened us and our deliverance from destruction during the night was taken as a good omen. We left Gothric and Abdiel at the head of the second formation and went to the front of the first, which was drawn up nearly against the foot of the hill. As we moved across the front rank, the enemy appeared over the brow of the hill, black against the pale light. Michael rode out in front of his troops and waited. I stood beside him, one hand gripping the stirrup leather. I watched Zareal ride down the hill towards us, holding his hand high above his head. Michael went forward to meet him.

"Hail, Michael," Zareal said, "and hail to the brown Chamiel. Michael, you make a brave show here and doubtless you will fight well. But for what? We have three times your numbers. We can crush and scatter you like cavings. Will you not, before it is too late, let us pass or, better still, join with us? When this whole kingdom is mine, I will not forget the favors and help given me. You would be well rewarded."

In the half-light I marked the whiteness of his teeth and I was lulled by the gentleness of his voice.

"No, Zareal. You will fight us here and be beaten back and driven from the Kingdom forever."

Then Zareal laughed and answered:

"You are very sure."

"The Lord's men are always sure," Michael said, reining his horse away.

When we returned to our ranks, a great silence fell over the field. While I was holding Michael's horse by the snaffle ring, I thought that this sudden hush was as though each side hesitated and was reluctant to let chaos loose. Between the two armies, from somewhere in the dewed grass, a lark rose in halting flight and singing. Against the heavy clouds which hung over us, it soon became invisible but its song was still clear and happy until drowned by the screech of Zareal's trumpets. A hoarse cry swept along their lines and they charged down upon us.

The sound of hooves pounded the air. I now saw that the enemy were clothed in black and on their chests were blazoned silver serpents. As they tore down upon us, I heard Zareal, who led them, lift his voice in some command. They came at us with wild screaming which made me shiver. The next instants were confusion; a mass of men and horses, some now riderless; men thrown to the ground; fierce screams, oaths, grunts and the terrible trampling of hooves. I was swept from Michael's side and thrown backwards to fall among our own men. I jumped up and saw that the enemy were right among our ranks. I looked for Michael and saw him not far off, urging the brothers to stand firm. I forced my way slowly towards him and came into a cleared space where he stood. As I ran to him, Zareal charged at Michael, whose back at that moment was turned. Zareal stretched out his arm against Michael at the very instant that I came between them. I lifted my staff with both hands and brought it down on the back of Zareal's hand. Michael turned and saw what had happened. There was no smile on Zareal's face as he spurred his horse at me. I stood where I was, waiting, but then Michael charged and headed him off and Zareal turned away and was lost in the turmoil.

A little later, the enemy horsemen withdrew.

Our ranks had been thinned and we had been pressed

back to the very bottom of the mountain. We re-formed and waited for the second assault. The air was hot and smelled of sweat and horse. Michael leaned down to me and said:

"Chamiel. You may go back to Gothric, if you wish."

I shook my head and took hold of his stirrup leather. He turned around to his men and looked at them for a moment before saying one word,

"Courage."

This time the black riders came in three waves, giving us no rest and we were forced back. I saw Zareal with one troop drive right through the weakest part of our front. But, instantly, Gothric led his men down upon Zareal, and forced them back. I found myself near Abdiel, who shouted something to me which I could not hear. A moment later I was knocked down and lay half conscious. One of the brothers picked me up, saying that this was no time or place in which to sleep. I recovered quickly and saw that our right flank had been forced so far back that the enemy would now be able to hem us in against the rocky side of the track. This was the position of which Michael had spoken before the battle and I saw that now he was withdrawing his men up the mountain and joining forces with Gothric. I caught up with Michael and heard him say:

"Brigit and Og should be here."

Zareal's onslaught was renewed and once again we were pushed upwards. Gothric brought some of the reserves down to patch the weakened places in our ranks. But now we had the advantage of the confined space in which to stand, where fewer men would be needed to hold the road. For this reason, too, Michael now dismounted and sent his horse to the rear. I stood by his side and he rested one hand on my shoulder, while he watched the enemy re-forming at the foot of the mountain.

"He is dismounting a number of them. Get Gothric."

I ran up through the lines and found Gothric with Abdiel who was lying on the ground. I told Gothric that Michael wanted him at once and asked what had happened to Abdiel.

"No time for that now. Get him to the baggage train. He'll tell you what happened when he comes to," Gothric answered, and strode off down the track.

I knelt by Abdiel and soon he opened his eyes and smiled.

"Are you all right? What happened?"

"Two of Zareal's men attacked me at the same time. I got one of them, but the other one rode me down and then Gothric arrived. I shall be all right."

He tried to stand but could not, even with my help. So I called to two brothers to help me and between us we carried him up into the pass and to the baggage train. When Abdiel saw me there, he said:

"You must get back. You can do nothing here. Go back to Michael."

So I left him and went down the mountain. Halfway down I stopped and watched the battle and I saw how Zareal had brought up more troops who beat with such weight against our thinning line that we were being driven back and back. Our line sagged and wavered and, then, in one place, I saw the enemy break through—a trickle of black among the white. But Michael held them and soon drove them out. He was wherever the line needed him, exhorting and encouraging and, at times, even joking. But in spite of his efforts and the stubborn valor of the brothers, our ranks were splitting and the whole line was splintering into little groups of struggling men. Michael, with one group, was almost surrounded. I heard, as I came nearer, Gothric bellow an order and watched him charge to Michael's aid. Zareal was waiting for such a move and immediately rushed a fresh section into the fight in order to surround both Gothric and Michael. But Gothric saw this action in time and signaled to the last

37

reserves to meet it. I went with them and, for a short while, in the shock of attack, I thought that we were holding them. But again, by a succession of sharp thrusts we were pressed back towards Michael and Gothric's men. I thought that now we would all be surrounded and I could hear Michael's voice behind me. I started to fight my way to him. A sweating brother beside me said, "We can't last much longer." I redoubled my efforts to get to Michael, knowing that now my place was beside him. The confusion was so great and the dust so thick that at times I could neither see nor hear. I found myself in a clear space where two horses had fallen and opposite me, as though he had been purposely waiting, stood Zareal. I stopped. I watched him smile and move towards me. I saw that he was saying something but only heard the word "knuckles." As he came closer, I raised my staff above my head. Then, above the din, flowed the smooth clear notes of a horn. High over us they were and Zareal looked up to the pass. There was Noral, a great horn at his lips, and the notes echoed down to us through the rocky gorge. Even at my first sight of him he was swallowed up by a force of galloping horsemen.

"Brigit," I shouted. When I turned, Zareal had gone.

Brigit led her men downwards at full gallop, her white hair flying and her crimson cloak streaming behind like wings. Her men wore crimson tunics so that the whole force was like a stream of blood down the mountain.

When they saw Brigit, the brothers raised a great cheer. She cut through Zareal's men, turned and charged them again from the rear.

I climbed onto a rock not only to see what was happening but to look for Michael. I saw that his small group of men had been joined now by others and were pressing the enemy slowly down the track. I saw Gothric in the center with a larger force holding Zareal and his men against the savage thrusts from Brigit. Gothric was the anvil and Brigit the hammer. But on the right flank, the enemy was

38

again breaking through and fresh men were being brought up to force the movement.

Then Og came with his gray men. At one moment I was watching the battle and thinking that in spite of Brigit we were still more than hard-pressed and the next. . . ."

Chamiel stopped because he was laughing.

"What was funny?" David asked.

'Og. You'll meet him one day. Og and his men had come through the pass and down the track. But nobody saw or heard them come. I didn't. They appeared beside me and there was Og. A small, round man with short, bristling red hair, a hooked nose, enormous black eyes below great terrifying black eyebrows. Like his men, he was dressed in gray and on his tunic was a red circle.

I looked up at him and smiled, because that is how he made me feel. He said:

"Where is Michael?"

I pointed and Og turned to look. After scanning the whole battlefield and its turmoil, he muttered:

"He doesn't want me there with him. Nor does that milk-sop Gothric, by the look of things."

Og spoke to one of his officers.

"We'll move against Zareal on that flank," he pointed, "where things look most interesting. That's where we're wanted. We'll have a chop at them from there and don't stop moving until you've driven every man of them over the Edges."

Then he stood and looked me up and down, his legs straddled and his fists clenched on his hips.

"Well, my pretty lad, what have you been doing?"

I told him. I told him all that had happened since the previous evening. At the end, he cleared his throat like a clap of thunder and said:

"Ridiculous bringing sucklings like you to a mix-up like

this. You only get in the way. What did that harum-scarum girl do when she got here?"

"Brigit?" I asked with a laugh.

"That's the one."

"She made a wonderful charge right through Zareal and then turned and charged him again. You should have seen her."

"Circus act," he answered and went off down the mountain.

Og and his men did what they said they would. They moved against Zareal and never stopped. They made no charge, but relentlessly pressed against the enemy, then through them and punched them further and further down the slopes. With shouting joy, I saw small groups of the enemy leaving the battle. The small groups became big groups which fled in all directions and Brigit's men were after them. Soon it became a rout and, for fear that I should be left behind, I ran down to join Michael. His eyes sparkled and he was laughing with Brigit. When I came up to them, Brigit looked hard at me and asked Michael who I was. Her face was small and round and her skin the color and texture of fine leather and it was wrinkled like crumpled parchment. But her eyes were soft blue. I stood between them and watched our men in full cry after the enemy. When Michael's horse was brought, Brigit said,

"Come. We must not let one of them escape."

I looked up at Michael and, without knowing what I said, whispered:

"Michael, I don't think I can run any more."

Brigit turned her head and smiled. Michael laughed and answered:

"Nor shall you," and he lifted me, as though I were a leaf, onto the saddle, in front of him.

Later, Brigit let me ride one of her horses and I rode between Brigit and Michael.

Michael kept his army from reckless pursuit and at

sundown we halted. By then we had driven them past the woods and onto the plain and it was decided to press on through the night so as not to lose touch with Zareal. By moonlight, we forded a river and soon after began to climb the downlands. I heard Brigit say to Michael:

"By dawn, we'll have them at the Edges."

And so we did. When the sun came up like a red ball, we drove them off the downs. Near a spinney of purple-flowered hibiscus, they made their last stand and Gothric and Og swept them over the Edges like dead flies.

I went to the very brink and watched them falling into the fog below and, perhaps because I was tired, I felt suddenly sad."

Chamiel stopped and there was silence in the room until David sat up and asked:

"What happened to Zareal?"

'Zareal? When he saw that all was lost, he tried to escape. But Michael and his men were waiting for him. They drove him over the Edges. He was the last to go and Michael told me that as he fell there appeared around Zareal a sheet of white flame which fell with him. Michael watched it until it was no bigger than a grain of bright sand.

After that, we went back to the baggage train, pitched tents and rested. On the way, we found many hundreds of holes in the ground where the cones had fallen. Some were as large as Lake Vassey and others no bigger than this room. From some, smoke and steam rose in great clouds as from the crater of Mount Hericulus, but in others you could look down and see through to the night. And I heard the wind echoing and groaning around and around, inside them. I was leaning over one of them with Og when he said to Gothric:

"These'll make good lookout posts. Keep an eye on those poor devils we've just thrown out. Job for you, my

41

boy." He gave a great bubbling laugh and smacked Gothric on the back.

That night, after Brigit and Og had said farewell to Michael and we were alone and quiet in the tent, I took Michael's book and began to read to him. After the first few lines, the carefully penned words grew blurred. Once, my head fell onto my chest. I remember that Michael got up from his blanket and carried me to mine. In the morning he said, smiling:

"I will not tell Xene that I read to myself last night."

We took two days to reach Michael's Court and on the last day's march Abdiel came and walked with me and we were on either side of Michael. When we reached the Heli woods, Noral sounded his bugle and at those happy notes the gates were thrown open and Gabriel came out to welcome us and the birds rose from the trees in full song.

Chamiel ended and after a little while David asked:

"Did you go with Michael to the Great Court?"

Chamiel smiled slowly.

"Yes. Indeed. I will tell you about that when I come again."

PART TWO

David, by the stream, turned his head quickly to watch a dragonfly disappear among the rushes. His eyes were intent on the spot where it had vanished; then, seeing no more of it, he went slowly down the bank to a clump of willows. He climbed into one and walked carefully, mouth open, arms raised, along a branch which hung over the water. Almost at the end of the branch he straddled it and leaned his body along it, his head resting on his hands. It was cool in the shade and quiet but for the slight shiver of the leaves or the occasional splash from a rising fish below. He stared into the moving stream and after a while turned his head sideways and closed his eyes.

"Chamiel?" he said in a half whisper, paused and repeated, "Chamiel?"

David idly lifted a hand and pushed his straight, yellow hair from his forehead and sat up. He stretched his arms and threw back his head.

"Chamiel?"

He climbed from the tree to sit on the bank's edge and dabbled his bare feet in the water.

When Chamiel came into the orchard, David looked around even though Chamiel's approach had been soundless. He got up and ran across the meadow's thick grass to the orchard. In the dappled shade Chamiel's figure was lost for seconds at a time, so that his presence might have been doubted. Yet David ran towards him without hesitation, and on reaching him he stopped. His head was slightly bent to one side, his arms hung limply and he was smiling. Chamiel stopped also and put his hands on the boy's shoulders, saying:

"Greetings David."

He took Chamiel's hand and they went down to the stream to sit in the willows' shade. David said:

"I've never called you before, even though I've sometimes wanted to."

"No," Chamiel answered, "I've come now because you called me and also because I have not been to you for so long."

"It's three years now."

Chamiel chuckled. "That is a long time for you. I've come too, among other things, to tell you that soon you will be a young man and that, as you grow up, so I shall come to you less often."

David was silent and thoughtful. At last he said with a frown:

"Will that be because I shall need you less and less as I get older?"

"No. It is not. You may well need me more. But you must learn to live your life alone, not relying on me or any others in your daily and earthly affairs. So, though I shall come to you from time to time until you come to us, you must not expect me often. Perhaps when you most need me—or think you do—I shall not come."

They talked and David asked Chamiel many questions and then for a while they were silent until the boy asked:

"You know that I have lots of dreams. At night I dream all kinds of dreams—sometimes they're about God and when I wake up I feel that He has made me dream that way for some special reason. D'you think that's right?"

Chamiel shook his head slowly.

"No, it's not right, David. God doesn't send dreams nor does He make you do anything. What you dream or think or do is of your own making."

"But we're always told that God is all powerful——

'Omniscient, omnipotent and omnipresent,' and makes all things happen?"

Chamiel laughed softly: "Listen. I will try to make this thing clear to you. Last time I promised that I would tell you of my going to the Great Court with Michael, didn't I?"

"Yes—did you meet the Lord?"

"Yes. I might have told you these things sooner but I do not think that you would have understood them. Now you will."

'After we had beaten Zareal and returned to Michael's Court, our lives went on as they had been before Zareal came to see Michael and Gabriel. We had extra duties, of course, and we were busy at first to make up for the time which we had lost.

One night, just before we went to sleep, Abdiel said:

"Gothric told me today that I'm going to the Great Court with him."

I sat up and my bed creaked so loudly that Abdiel turned over and asked:

"What's the matter?"

"Michael told me that I'd go with him."

"When?"

"When? When the war was over."

"No. When did he tell you?"

"Oh—the morning of the day on which we reached the Kopal. I told you he took me up the mountain side and showed me the hill with the Great Court on it. That's when he told me I'd go there with him."

"Then you will," Abdiel answered sleepily. "You'll go before we do and I expect you'll be away longer, too, because Michael will probably make some visits."

"Visits? To whom?"

"Oh, I should think Brigit and Og and possibly to Burns, who looks after the new entrants, and to Mithandrwe——"

Abdiel stopped abruptly and I heard him giggling.

"What are you laughing at? Who's Mithandrwe?"

"He's in the fruitlands now—looking after things there. He used to be here. Michael loves him because he makes Michael laugh. He's always full of jokes that aren't really funny—except to him and that's what makes people laugh. Besides, he's terribly inquisitive and wants to know exactly what's happening everywhere. If you don't tell him what he wants to know, he tries all kinds of ways to get it out of you. And that used to be quite a game with some of us when he was here. He's always grumbling, too. But no one pays attention to it. He doesn't mean it. It's just a habit. He's very kind, especially to us."

I said "Oh" and lay back. I wondered when Michael would tell me about his visit. I watched a vine of honeysuckle moving across the open window and heard Abdiel fall asleep and saw the moon climb over the window sill and light our room and then I went to sleep.

Some days later, when I was with Sassis, a young one, in the South Garden, I heard Xene's thin voice calling for me. I stopped reading and got up from the grass, saying, "I wonder what he wants?" although I guessed what it was. I ran down the paths lined with red and white camellias until I came, panting, to the gate where Xene was standing.

"I sent for you. Did you not get my message?"

"No, Xene."

He clucked.

"Well, it can't be helped. You are to go to the Great Court with Michael tomorrow. You start in the morning. You'd better come now to collect the book."

When we were in his room, he pointed, saying, "There is new clothing for you, which you will need at the Great Court and later when you are the guest of those whom Michael will visit. Here is Michael's book. You may not be able to read to him each night because you will retire at different times and at the Great Court you may not see him until he takes you to the Lord. But do not let that be an excuse for not reading to him when it is at all possible."

"No, Xene."

"Remember, too, that you are to be the guest of his friends and, because you went with Michael to the war, you are in no way better than any other. You will be modest always and say nothing of the things which you did and little of the things which you saw, unless you are asked."

"Yes."

"Tomorrow, an hour before sunrise, you will go to the stables where all will be ready for you and you will bring the horses to the Court steps and wait there for Michael." Xene paused and drew in his breath. "The Lord has asked that you should go to Him. You will return here therefore with more wisdom and you will no longer be a young one—but in no way considering yourself above any others."

"No."

"Go now. I shall see you in the morning."

"Thank you. Xene?"

"Yes?"

"Is it long since you were at the Great Court?"

"Yes. Yes. Long in time, but not in memory."

It was half light and the air was fresh when we set out. The brothers, as well as many of the young ones, had crowded into the forecourt to bid us farewell and to wish us a happy journey. Then, when we reached the gateway, Noral sounded a long fanfare on his trumpet and we rode through the gateway and turned towards the rising sun, following a road around one side of the Court.

We went by the garden fields where the workers stopped their work to wave to us. I looked back and saw the ring-doves circling and dipping in a soft, white greeting over the Court roofs.

Soon we came into the marshes, where the sunlight was

reflected from the still, wide pools and I had to close my eyes against the glare. We went in single file here, Michael leading the way along the narrow track. Once he stopped to talk with some reed cutters who had hailed him. We came out of this cold country onto the higher lands where the earth was black. It was strange land, neither flat nor hilly, but swollen by long, gentle curves, like the sea still grumbling after a great storm. The ground seemed to flow away from us on all sides to the pale horizon. It was cornland, white with barley, dusky gold with wheat, yellow with oats, muddy with rye, and slowly moving over all were the black shadows of the clouds. The few trees were flat-topped and bent like reapers.

We were nearly all day in crossing the cornlands and saw no one. But, by evening, we were near the forests and, even before I saw the first trees, I told Michael that I could smell the scent of oak and balsam.

When we reached the forests, we followed a ride which led to the north. It was quiet here after the continual brushing of the wind through the corn. Now, the silence was broken only by a crackling stick under the horses' hooves or, when I spoke, by the sudden shrillness of my voice. By dusk, we came to a wide clearing at the far end of which was a wooden house with the door open. Black against the orange light from within was the figure of a woman standing on the threshold. As soon as she saw us, she started forward and when Michael reached her, said:

"Welcome, Michael. I had heard of your journey and hoped that you would come this way."

"Thank you, Margaret. We shall gladly rest here."

Margaret spoke to me. "You are welcome, too, Chamiel."

"Thank you," I answered.

She told me that the stables were at the back of the house and added:

"Marla is there now."

50

When I had stabled the horses, I recrossed the small yard. A girl appeared through the gloom and said:

"Are you Chamiel?"

"Yes. You're Marla?"

"Yes. We thought you'd come this way. Michael usually does when he goes to the Great Court. Margaret has been excited even since she heard that you were journeying."

When we reached the house, I asked where Michael was to sleep and Marla took me to his room.

"You'll have to sleep in the houseroom. It may be hot, but you can leave the door open," she said.

I took Michael's book from the pouch and laid it by the bed.

"What book is that?"

"Michael's. He reads it each night. Sometimes, I read it to him."

Holding the lamp above her head, she leaned over my shoulder. The light shone not only on the book but on her hair as well. It was fine and so pale gold that it seemed almost white and was cut short to a little below her ears. Her eyes were large and dark brown.

"Let me see," she said. So I opened the book and watched her eyes moving along the lines, her lips slightly open. After a moment's reading, she said:

"It makes you feel happy and sad, both at the same time—like a sunset."

In the houseroom Margaret and Michael were already sitting at a long, wooden table placed against one of the room walls. Marla sat down at one end and Margaret told me to take my place at the other end. From here I could see out through the doorway to the trees, their tops black against the blue night.

During our meal, Margaret asked Michael to tell the story of his fight against Zareal, which he did. I remember Marla's eyes, wide open and shining when he told of the fire cones, and the sudden snatch of breath from Mar-

51

garet at the description of the wind which scattered them. When he ended, Marla said:

"Have you brought your staff with you, Chamiel?"

I shook my head and Margaret rebuked her:

"For what would he want a staff now?"

Later, I went to Michael's room and read to him. I think that he was asleep before I had finished reading, because he said nothing to me. I waited for a while but he gave no sign. So I blew out the lamp and went to my bed. I lay, not wanting to sleep, and thought of the past day's happenings and then of how the next day would be. I looked out through the faint blue square of the doorway and listened to the whispers from the forest and to the sudden winds that scuffled through the trees. Before I slept I thought that I heard a fox barking and the sounds echoing away and away into the distance.

The sky was still drowsy when Marla woke me. While I dressed, she laid the fire and lighted it. I saw that she was wearing a short, blue leather jacket with many flowers embroidered on the front of it. Beneath the jacket was a white blouse and her short skirt of dark blue leather was belted with a wide red belt. Her feet were bare.

We went to the stables and she helped me feed and groom the horses. Afterwards, she said:

"Come and see something."

"What?"

"Come and see," and she took my hand and pulled me out of the yard. She led me to another clearing in the forest where the red earth had been ploughed and cultivated. By the clear light I saw row upon row of seedling trees. Marla took me across the rows, telling me what kind of trees they were as we came to them. We stopped at a long, wooden shed. Marla pushed the door open and called me inside.

"We look after all this," she said.

All around the shed were racks and small bins in which the tree seeds were stored. I asked:

"You gather all these?"

"A lot. Yes. The woodmen bring others. We sort and put them into the right racks. Margaret and I sow a great many of the seeds and then we look after them until it's time for them to go out into the forest." She stopped talking and went outside and stood looking up into the pale sapphire sky. "I'm sorry to see them go," she added.

We went back through the clearing and when she stopped to look at one of the treelings, I said:

"Marla, I ought to go back to Michael."

"Not yet. Come and swim in the brook. I go every morning except in the winter."

She laughed at me because I found the water cold. But I swam faster than she did. Then we returned to the house. On the way there she asked:

"What d'you do at Michael's Court?"

"Learn."

"What?"

I told her and after a little thought, she asked:

"What will you do when you finish learning?"

"What will you do when you're grown up?" I answered.

She suddenly laughed and skipped away from me. Then returned because I had stopped and was smiling at her.

"Well, what?" she repeated.

"I shall be with Michael, I hope. Perhaps doing some of his work."

"Will you go to the Great Court then?"

"I don't know. Would you like to?"

She put her hands behind her head and looked up to the sky.

"No. I'm not made for those things. I hope I shall stay here with Margaret and the trees and the brook and the woodmen and the smell of leaves and the night noises." She paused and then added, "——the rain dripping

53

through the trees and the great winter winds which bend the tall trees like harp strings." She stopped, looked at me and said, "D'you understand?"

"Yes. Very well. But won't you have a ward one day?"

"Perhaps. Even if I do, I shall live here when I come back with it."

"It?" I asked.

"Well, a boy," and she ran on and I followed.

After I had saddled the horses, I led them out into the yard. Marla was looking at the silver patterns on the headband of Michael's horse.

"Marla——Hold the horses for a moment, will you?"

While she held them, I undid the gold clasp which fastened the neck of my tunic.

"What are you doing?"

"Will you have this?" I asked and handed her the clasp. She looked at me without moving and said:

"Who gave it to you?"

"Brigit—on the way back from the Edges," and I put it into her hand.

She looked down at the clasp which shone in her open palm, hesitated and then said, "Thank you. I have nothing for you."

"That doesn't matter," I answered.

"Will you come back this way?"

"I don't think so. We're going on to see Brigit and Og and Mithandrwe."

Soon after that, we rode through the forest. At the time when we set out, the day had been clear and hot and the dark coolness of the trees had been welcome. But in the mid-morning the sun left us and gray, heavy clouds swept away the blueness. The air became hotter and the trees now seemed to surround us with their warm, moist breath. I saw Michael glancing at the sky, but I said nothing. As we came to the top of a steep rise, at a point where four rides crossed and made a frost pattern, a sudden wind swept over the tree tops and turned them from dark green to a quivering gray.

"It's like the wind in the Kopal," I shouted.

"This one will wet us," Michael answered. He was right. For the gale died as quickly as it had come and then we heard the sighing of rain and watched it draping towards us over the forest.

We sheltered among the trees and Michael dismounted.

"Chamiel."

"Yes?"

"You gave your gold clasp to Marla?"

"Yes."

"What will you say if Brigit asks where it is?"

"I will tell her that I gave it to Marla."

"Brigit may not like that," Michael said and he came to me, putting one hand on the back of my saddle. He smiled and saw that I was troubled and I asked:

"What shall I do?"

Michael put his other hand onto mine which was holding the reins and then turned his hand upwards, opening it so slowly that I thought his fine-boned fingers were like the opening petals of a flower, and its center was yellow with the gold clasp.

"Look, Chamiel."

But I had seen already and Michael laughed at my astonishment and gladness. I put my arm around his neck because I could say nothing.

"Margaret brought it to me," he said. "Because she knew that it would be difficult for you if Brigit asked where it was. I told her that when we reached the Great Court, we would have a clasp made and that you would bring it to Marla when we got back."

"Thank you, Michael."

We rode down the long ride watching the rain sweeping over the country before us and feeling the sun's warmth on our backs once more. The horses' hooves squelched in

55

the sodden grass; the leaves shone with diamonds and when I said this to Michael, he answered:

"And they squander them on the ground below."

Now we saw that we would soon leave the forest lands and come into a country of small, softly rounded hills. Michael pointed, saying:

"There is the cattle country and there, at the edge of the forest—see?—at the foot of the hill, is Corvan."

"Where they make all the things from the forest wood?"

"Yes—Hail, Karel."

"Hail, Michael."

I was startled by the strange voice and turned in the saddle to see a group of men who had come from among the trees and who now stood by the edge of the ride. They were dressed in leather jackets of dark green. The jackets ended at their waists and were buttonless, hanging open to show their brown and hairy chests. Their breeches were of black leather and fastened with yellow thongs below their knees. Their legs were clothed in thick, green, woolen stockings and on their feet were heavy black sandals with no buckle fastenings. Karel, who had greeted Michael, stood in the front of the group. He wore a stained leather hat, and in the yellow cord twisted around the hat to form a crown for it, was stuck a brown and white eagle's feather. All these men had either axes, hooks or mattocks. Some rested these tools over their shoulders while others rested them on the ground. Karel said to me:

"Greetings, Chamiel," and he smiled. I noticed that his beard was patched with white hairs.

"We heard of your coming, Michael," he went on, "and have waited here, wishing to see you."

The woodmen crowded around us and we dismounted. I led the horses a little way off and stayed there, but Karel called:

"Hi, boy, come back here. We want to know what Zareal's knuckles look like."

At this there was a loud shout of laughter. So I tied the horses to a tree and went back to the group. Michael stood in the middle of these men, who all were swarthy and tall and bearded. Yet Michael stood taller than all of them and the sunlight shining on his gray hair turned it to silver and his white clothes gleamed against the dark clothing of the woodmen. As I stood and watched, I suddenly knew that these men not only admired but loved Michael and that they would have come to greet him on any journey which he might have made through their territory.

Michael told them briefly the story of the war, and when he spoke of my set-to with Zareal the woodmen turned to me and Karel patted my shoulder. But not knowing what to say, I was silent. Then, after Michael had finished speaking, Karel said:

"When we heard that you had marched to Blendinah, we left the forests and hurried to join you. But by the time we got to the Kopal, you were gone. We marched during the night and the sky was red with fires and the earth trembled as though a giant were shaking it and against the darkness we saw many bursts of flame. We have been told that this was an evil of Zareal's making against which the Lord sent a mighty wind and destroyed this wickedness."

Then Michael told them of the flying cones and said that I had warned the camp of their coming and when he stopped there was silence and I heard one or two of the woodmen muttering to themselves. Soon after that we said farewell and Karel made me promise to return. He said that I should come to live with them so that I could warn them of forest fires.

At midday, we reached Corvan where all the wood mills had stopped work and the people thronged the streets, hailing and cheering Michael, who smiled and

57

thanked them for their welcome. Amid the hubbub I sometimes heard my own name called.

We were led to Amry's house and rested there. When we were refreshed, Amry, who was large, well-bellied and red-faced, took us into the market square on one side of which a platform had been built. We were brought to this platform and from it could see over all the crowded square. Many people looked from the open windows of the houses. Then Amry told the people that Michael would tell them the story of the war and how the Black Angel had been cast out. At this there was such cheering that Michael could not at first be heard but at last he began his story and through its long telling there was no sound or movement from the listeners and I watched the roof shadows move a yard across the slates before he had ended. There was an even deeper silence when he stopped, until one man, whose bald head shone in the sunlight and who was close to the platform, lifted his arm and cried:

"Let us thank the Lord. Let us thank Michael."

At that all the people sang and the great sound swelled and echoed from the walls and I could hear nothing but the volume of their joy. At the end, the people surged closer to the platform, again cheering Michael, and he waved to them. Suddenly, from somewhere among the crowds, I heard a chanting of voices calling, "Chamiel, Chamiel," and the sound spread across the square until it became the pounding of a great hammer. Michael took my hand and brought me to the front of the platform and Amry moved a bench for me to stand on so that everyone could see. I lifted my hand, smiled and tears ran down my cheeks and Michael put his arm around me. He called for silence and said:

"Soon Gothric and Abdiel will come and from them you will hear more—things which I have not had time to relate—for by tonight we must be at the Great Court. So

58

now Chamiel and I thank you for your love and wish you well."

Then we left the platform and passed slowly through the heat of the people until we came into the cool of Amry's house. He gave us drink and we said farewell and rode through the happy crowds and left the bustle of Corvan. Then, but for the bleat of sheep, it was quiet. Michael said:

"You are tired?"

I nodded.

"Strong feelings are more wearying than battle."

And I laughed suddenly and said yes.

We rode on until we came to a stream and Michael looked at the sun and said:

"We will rest here for a little so that we may reach the Court refreshed, for it is not far off."

So I took the horses and watered them and tied them in the shade of the alders by which we had stopped. Michael lay on the grass and I gave him my sheepskin coat and brought the horn book to him because he asked for it. While he read, I threw off my tunic and sandals and plunged into the warm water. There I idled until Michael called that it was time to go.

We went by a winding sheep meadow, sometimes following the flank of a small hill and sometimes riding straight up and over the short-grassed hills. Everywhere, the fields were dotted with cattle and sheep. The shepherds waved to us and the drovers, of whom many were girls, called greetings as we passed. Then, when the sun was in its last quarter and the air had become cooler, we rode up a stony track bounded on both sides by dead bracken. I chanced to look at Michael's face and saw that he was smiling.

"Why are you smiling, Michael?"

"You will know soon," he answered.

We came to the crown of the hill and I suddenly saw what lay ahead. I stopped short. Michael turned to me.

"You see?" he said.

In front of us rose the long, rounded hill which I had seen from the Noon Mountains. But now it was not glittering as though set in precious stones. Each house was in a garden and both gardens and buildings mounted in a gentle, terraced curve up the side of the hill. The forms of the trees and shrubs, their colors and the colors of the many flowers hid the houses so that only their roofs could be seen. In the evening's light these were now turned to the color of dull silver.

The buildings were in two rows and between them was a wide, grassy walk which led to the summit and to the Great Court itself. The Great Court was built of a white stone and it was circular, its outer edge pillared to support the domed roof which was of crystal. The whole of this wonderful building gathered within itself the day's light and radiated it like an immense aureole.

Around the Court lay the gardens. Some were lawns, some were walled and some terraced. I caught a glimpse of wide steps and paths leading away to other grounds which were hidden by the shoulder of the hill and I now saw the double rank of weeping pear trees, gray-leaved and circling, as Xene had once told me, the whole Court.

I saw all these things with wonder and Michael spoke softly.

"I have seen this many, many times. Yet each time it is new and more beautiful and so it always will be."

I did not know if he was speaking to me or to himself and I made no answer.

I had been excited from the moment when Xene had first told me that I was to go to the Great Court. But now, seeing it so fair and so close and realizing that I was to be taken to its Lord, I suddenly became anxious as I had been when I first saw the Black Angel's armies. Once again I wished to turn away.

Michael and I stayed looking over the hill in silence for

a long while. But, when our horses fretted, Michael said:

"They have seen us."

I looked where he was pointing and saw that at the bottom of the hill where the green walk began, several white-clad figures were gathering. We rode slowly down the hill and they, seeing us moving, came toward us.

"Chamiel?" Michael spoke quietly.

"Yes, Michael?"

"Is your heart beating fast?"

"Yes."

Michael chuckled.

"So is mine. Every time that I reach this spot and ride down the hill I am filled with awe, although I know that at the instant when I reach the foot of the hill all this fear will vanish and I shall be filled with peace. So it will be with you at the moment when we dismount." He paused and then added, "For all walk up to the Great Court. When we reach it, you will no longer be with me as my squire and possibly I shall not see you until we go to the Lord together."

"When?"

"Tomorrow morning."

"Oh."

Michael laughed, saying:

"This is no battle, boy. Come."

At the foot of the hill we were greeted by the brothers and the horses were led away. While two of the brothers were speaking with Michael, a third one with a boy at his side approached me.

"Welcome, Chamiel," he said and asked of our journey, about which I told him briefly. Then he said:

"This is Basil, who will look after you while you are here." At this, Basil came forward and we greeted each other. We were of the same height and age, but his hair was red and his skin very pale and his eyes were large and honey-colored. There was no time for talk between us then because Michael, with a tall, thin brother beside him, had started to walk up the hill. Basil said:

"Quick. You and Michael in front and I and Timothy walk behind."

So I turned hurriedly to catch up with Michael, and as I reached his side there came down to us through the quiet air the sound of pealing bells.

We were at the start of the way up to the Great Court, which, as I've told you, is lined on either side with dwellings of all sizes, but all built from the same kind of stone. In the front of each house were plots with flowers growing in them and beds with flower-covered shrubs and in the spaces between each of the dwellings were intertwined limes. At intervals, on either side of the walk, grew orange trees, now heavy with yellowing fruit, while on some of the house-porches were hung baskets from which trailed brightly flowering plants, and in others were stone sinks or vases and in them grew clipped box, yews or purple saramite. I saw that many of the walls were covered by roses, or jasmines or verbenas and blood-red vines or flame flowers and on some were the blue-trumpeted morning glories.

As soon as the bells started to ring, the doors opened and men, women and young ones came out and stood by the wayside and greeted us. Not with shouts and cheers, as at Corvan, but with smiles and waving hands. I watched Michael and acknowledged their salutes as he did.

Near the crown of the hill, the grassy way broadens and just before it reaches the Great Court it becomes a wide lawn leading right to the Court itself. Here there are no buildings but only four dark, drooping cedars which make a square of shade and, beyond them, the lines of weeping pear trees. When we reached the lawn, I looked up and put a sudden hand on Michael's sleeve.

"Michael—look at the roof."

The setting light shone through the crystal roof whose

color had now changed from that of a diamond to the soft iridescence of a pearl. I stopped in wonder. Michael said:

"Its color changes with every change of light. Every hour and every day. Like the sky itself, the roof is never as it was a moment before."

As we crossed the soft lawn, Basil came to my side and Timothy walked with Michael. I did not speak. I felt that Basil did not expect me to. So we passed through the sudden coolness beneath the cedars and then through the pear trees and came to the entrance to the Court. There was a flight of three shallow steps leading up to the colonnaded enclosure and, when we touched the bottom step, Gabriel came forward to the top step and with him a small, stout man dressed in a long white robe, around whose waist was a sash of scarlet cloth and from this, at his right side, hung a bunch of clinking keys.

"That's Ragna—the Court Steward," Basil whispered.

If you asked me to describe my clearest memory of Gabriel, then I would choose that evening and that moment with the sharp remembrance of his wise figure standing at the portals of the Great Court and the radiance from the roof suffusing the precincts and making him part of all its warmth. I wondered if it was this beautiful light or his pleasure in having Michael with him again which kindled his face. Perhaps one as much as the other.

We were taken to a vestibule on the right side of the entrance and there corded patinas were brought to us and our sandals removed. After that, Ragna took Michael away and Gabriel went with him. I asked Basil the reason for the patinas.

"For quietness. Come on. I'm going to take you to Chai."

"Chai?"

"She's in charge of the young ones and looks after some of the guests, especially if they can't look after themselves." He paid no attention to my answer but hurried

63

on. "She's not as awesome as she'd like us to think her—not that I have much to do with her now. She comes from the Sealands."

"Where all the colored brothers are?"

"Yes."

After a pause, I said, "There aren't any gates here, are there?"

"No. Anyone can come in who wants to. But most try to make some arrangements with Ragna first."

"We've gates at Michael's."

"They're only to keep you in," Basil answered and I made a face at him.

"The only time they've ever been closed was during the war," I said.

We left the vestibule. He led me through another doorway and we came into the Great Hall. It was circular and, like the Court's outer edge, colonnaded. The slender columns were set on narrow plinths, the stems round and tapered, and the capitals were arched like amaryllis leaves, supporting a wide gallery off which I saw many doorways. I thought for a moment that I was standing below the sky, but, when I looked around the hall, I realized that the crystal roof refracted all the sunset's brilliance onto the stone floor, walls and pillars. Except for a round, shallow pool in the center, fringed with many-colored primrose, there was no need for other ornament.

We stood and looked into the water of the pool and Basil said:

"You never can tell what this hall will look like from one moment to another because of the changing light. But it's always beautiful, even in the dull winter days— the whole place sometimes looks as though it had been made from pewter."

He took me up to the gallery. From there we stared down at the pool. In the last clearness before dark, the water was like a shining beryl stone.

Basil led me down a long stairway until we reached a

curtained opening. Lifting the curtain, he signed for me to go into the room beyond. The room was filled with clothing of all kinds, much of it stacked on shelves which lined three of the walls. The fourth wall was of glass. As I came in, the silhouette of a small woman came from behind a pile of clothes heaped on the table. I could only see the outline of her body because the window was behind her.

"Chamiel?" she asked.

"Yes."

"Welcome. I am Chai. You are late. Basil, why were you so long in bringing our guest? Now he will be hurried in his washing and dressing."

Her voice was small, sweet with the cadences of little hand bells.

"I think that we talked too long in the vestibule and stayed too long looking at the Hall. Sorry, Chai."

"Go now and return for Chamiel in time to take him to Refectory."

Basil disappeared and Chai lighted a lamp, saying:

"Come along."

In that light, which suddenly darkened the window and made it a glass, I saw Chai for the first time. She was little taller than I and very thin. Her cheekbones slanted sharply to a small, cleft chin and they jutted from her cheeks so that there were shadows below them. Her eyes were large, soft and purple-brown like the heather on Harrivay and they were lozenge shaped. Her skin was yellow and in the lamplight seemed powdered with gold dust. She had her hair cut short about her ears and it was black even against the blackness of the window. I stood looking at her, paying no attention to her words. For when I remembered what Basil had said about her awesomeness, I was filled with quick compassion for her and I smiled at her as she stood with one hand on the door curtain and the other holding the wavering lamp. She stopped and only her shadow moved gently on the curtain and I wondered what she was thinking. When I followed her, she put out her hand and touched my hair with her fingertips. Her hand smelled of distant stephanotis.

Chai took me to my room, adjoining which was the washing room. She pointed to it.

"Go in and bathe. I will bring you fresh clothes from your pack."

I lay in the heated water while she took away my traveled clothes and left me fresh ones. She rubbed me with oils and combed my hair. These were attentions which I had never had and I was a little lost. Chai asked me about Michael's Court, about our journey, about Gothric and Abdiel; and then she told me about the land from which she came, where it was summer all year round."

Chamiel paused and said to David:

"You may wonder why I tell you all these things?"

"Because Chai didn't usually take all that trouble with guests?"

"No. That is not the reason," Chamiel answered. "Although at Michael's Court there was the gray-headed Wendien, who had charge of the youngest ones in much the same way as Chai, we had to do everything for ourselves and were not waited upon except at table. Basil said that this was the same for the young ones at the Great Court."

Then Chamiel went on with his story.

'My room at the Great Court was like the one which I shared with Abdiel. There were the same white walls and narrow bed with brightly colored blankets and the same little chest made from jarra wood and with holly-wood handles. Like Chai's workroom, one wall was of glass for a window and it was opened wide. But, unlike my room at Michael's, on the white ceiling was a roundel painted in the clearest, brightest colors, showing a bird and the roundel's frame was a gold circle. I asked Chai what kind of a bird it was. She laughed:

"You really don't know?"

"No."

"That is a bird of Paradise." Then she went on, "Hurry Chamiel. It is now nearly time and our guests must not be late."

At that moment Basil returned and he took me down long flights of stairs to the Refectory.

In the middle of this room were two half-round tables and the room was lighted by candles set on these tables and in niches in the walls. On both sides of the table were half-round benches. The room, like all those which I had seen, was without ornament but for a large, golden circle on the white ceiling. Around the circle were painted twining sprays of passion flowers. The walls of the room were white, but the floor was dark with polished panga panga.

As I came into the entrance way, Basil took my wrist and said under his breath:

"We wait here."

We stood at the top of three wide steps which led down into the room. Ragna came forward from among the groups of brothers and led me to my table place and Basil sat on my left side and Ragna on my right. I saw that Chai, who must have come by some other way, was seated on Ragna's right side. When the four of us were at the table, the brothers took their places. I noticed that there were a number of young ones among them and, when we were seated, I asked Basil:

"Do the young ones always have meals here?"

"No. Only on special occasions," and he grinned at me.

I asked Ragna if either Gabriel or Michael would come. He shook his head and answered.

"No. They are with the Lord."

"Will I be able to see Michael tonight?"

"Is it important?"

I told him about Michael's book. He answered with a slight smile:

"I will take it to him for you."

I shook my head.

"Very well, then, we will go to Michael's room after this."

At the end of the meal, all the company rose and a bearded brother, wearing a dark crimson tunic with a white collar, intoned a prayer of thanks. Then we sat down, remaining in absolute silence for some moments. Many of the brothers had their eyes closed. Ragna rose, broke the silence and said:

"Brother Chamiel is with us for the first time. We ask him to tell us the story of Michael's battle against Zareal."

So then, when Ragna was seated, I stood and told the whole story which I have told you. When I ended and had sat down, the bearded brother got up.

"We will remember this night," he said. "We shall sing of Michael and Gothric, of Brigit and Og, of Abdiel and Chamiel and all the brothers who fought. We will make a song of how they vanquished evil and the song will be sung at this season for evermore. Now we thank Chamiel who has told us this story in a child's voice and with a child's voice we will give thanks for deliverance."

To the accompaniment of a stringed instrument, one of the young ones sang and the room was filled with clear, appealing notes and I thought that it was the happiest sound I had ever heard. When the singer ended, the bearded brother leaned towards him and said so that all could hear:

"Well done, well done, John."

And we clapped hands for him. Then the singer lighted a silver lamp and brought it to me and I rose and took it from his hands and thanked him. Basil, Ragna and I left

68

the table. I carried the lamp. On the top entrance step we turned and faced into the room. All the company was standing in a circle around the tables and when we turned to them, they gave a great shout, bidding me "Good rest and farewell." I thanked them for their love and wishes, recalling the words which Michael had spoken to the people of Corvan. Then Ragna and Basil took me to my room and Basil left me. I asked Ragna if I could go to Michael and walked at Ragna's side through the silence of many corridors, coming at last to Michael's room, which was on the opposite segment of the Court. We found that the room was empty. I heard Ragna mutter something about important business that should keep him so late, but all I said was "It's no bigger than mine."

"Why should it be?"

I looked at the roundel on the ceiling. It was bordered in gold like the one in my room, but within the border were painted the head and shoulders of a man. Ragna laughed at my astonishment.

"You know him?"

"It's Michael."

After that Ragna left me, saying that he could wait no longer, having other things to see to. I took the book and, sitting on a small stool, began to read.

Michael woke me by lifting me from the stool. I stared at him sleepily. He was laughing softly.

"I've kept you a long time, Chamiel, I'm afraid. You need not have waited."

"Michael—you will come with me tomorrow?"

"Of course. I have said I would."

His face became suddenly grave. "It is possible that I shall have to stay here for a time."

"And can I stay, too?"

"I do not think so. But tomorrow I shall know for certain."

"Has something happened? Something bad?"

He looked down at me and answered slowly:

"Yes and No. You will know tomorrow."

I read to him then for a little while, although he said that I need not. When I had finished, he came back with me to my room. As I got under the blankets, he said almost in a whisper:

"Even Heaven can be troubled without end."

He left and I snuffed the candle and lay looking into the night. I smelled the heavy sweetness of jasmine and the Court was silent.

I woke when the dawn was only a thin, white line in the far darkness and I stood by the open window until all the birds were singing. Then I went back to my bed and slept until Chai woke me. She brought food, and after I had dressed she combed my hair and spoke again of her own country. I asked her questions and said:

"Perhaps I shall go there one day?"

"You will," she answered. "You will travel to many lands—some beyond this Kingdom."

I looked at her wonderingly.

"You are surprised that I should know?"

"Yes."

"When you have been at the Great Court for so long as I have and have cared for so many of the young ones, you understand them quickly and often you know how, when their time comes, they will serve the Lord."

"I will serve by journeying?"

"By journeys to strange places, by wisdom of tongue, by love."

"I shall see Him today."

"Yes. In a few moments."

Before I could say more, Basil came. He greeted Chai and then said:

"I am to take you to Michael first. After, I shall not see you again till you come from the Lord. Then I shall be waiting for you in the Great Hall."

I thanked Chai for all her kindness to me and said farewell to her. Then I left the room with Basil.

When I was alone with Michael, he turned gravely from looking out of the window of his room and spoke:

"Remember one thing, Chamiel. The Lord Himself has asked that you should come to Him. It is neither I nor any other who has asked on your behalf. It is His own wish and so He has pleasure in expecting you."

"I understand."

"Before we go, I must tell you this. I now know that I shall have to stay here for some extra days. If all is well, I shall then visit Brigit, Og and Mithandwre. If you were to wait here for me, you would be kept too long from your duties. For both our sakes, I am sad that you will not be with me. But you must return to my Court to ask Gothric to come here as soon as he can with Abdiel. There is no need for you to hurry over your journey home, but do not delay unduly."

As he spoke the last words, I saw that he was smiling. He put his hand into the blouse of his tunic and took out a small, olivewood box which he gave to me.

I took the box and looked at it. Michael said:

"This is something that you may wish to have on your journey."

Then, as I still stared at it, he said:

"The box will open."

I opened it. On a padded lining of black material shone a gold clasp in the shape of a small tree and the leaves of the tree were so skillfully crafted that they seemed to quiver as if lifted by a little breeze. All I could say was:

"It's so beautiful."

He put his hand on my shoulder, saying:

"Now we must go."

We left the Court through a doorway on the side opposite to that which we had entered on the previous day. We crossed the circling lawn and passed between the weeping pear trees and then followed a path of white flagstones, their crevices filled with a small red-leaved plant which

71

scented the air each time the leaves were disturbed. This path led us to a flight of steps. From them I saw the gardens which lay before us. They stretched in terraces almost to the foot of the hill. The last flight ended in a paved circle at the center of which was a large pool, overflowing into a small brook that twisted out of sight among clumps of trees.

At the end of every flight of steps and flanking them on each side were planted two golden yews. The terraces on either side of the steps were paved and in the middle of the paving were long, narrow beds filled with flowering plants.

Michael had paused at the top of the steps. I think that he did this so that I should have time to see all that lay below. I said:

"Where is He?"

Michael laughed and answered:

"If you came here looking for Him by yourself, you might be many hours searching. But I will wager that He is over there." He pointed to his right where the terraces ended under archways formed in a dividing wall and separating the terraces from the adjoining garden. Hanging from the middle of every archway was a basket from which trailed blood-red and yellow flowers.

Michael went down to the third terrace. I lingered for an instant and then ran to join him. We passed by one of the beds, planted with silver-leaved, blue-flowering grisnea and the air was sweet with their fragrance. Through the archway, we came into a square, walled garden, where fruit trees were trained in all manner of shapes. These trained trees were planted against the walls or on the three edges of the four plots into which the garden was divided. The division was made by two paths. In the middle of the four plots were still other trees, but these grew naturally and were not trained into shapes.

We reached the point where the two paths crossed. Michael stopped and said softly:

"There He is."

I followed the direction of his eyes and put my hand into his at which he looked down at me and I think in that moment some of his joy was given to me. We went forward slowly and the Lord came towards us.

"Greetings, Michael. Greetings, Chamiel," He said.

I knelt before Him and said, "Greetings, Lord," and He laughed gently and put His hand on mine and said:

"Stand up. There is no need to kneel to me."

We walked on either side of Him, between the apple and pear trees and there was silence until He said:

"The apples will be good this season—well colored and well ripened and, unless we have bad storms, well harvested. The pears, too. This should be an excellent year for them—if the wasps leave them alone."

He stopped, went to one of the trees and, after carefully feeling two or three of the fat pears, picked and gave me one.

We moved slowly up the hill while He spoke to Michael and we came to a stone arbor at the end of the path. He said:

"Let us sit here, for it is already hot."

He and Michael sat on the stone seat within the arbor and I sat between them. Then the Lord said to me:

"Chamiel, do you know why I have asked you to come to see me?"

"No, Lord."

"To thank you for your help in our fight against Zareal."

"But I did no more than part of my duty."

"I have heard differently," He said. "I have heard that Zareal's knuckles were sore; that someone saw his armies from afar and so enabled Michael to get his men into position in time; that someone gave warning of the fire cones. Are these things so?"

I glanced towards Michael and saw that he was laughing to himself and I answered:

"Yes. They are. But anyone would have done just as I did. And Og told me that sucklings like I—only got in the way——"

At this they both laughed and the Lord said:

"That was only Og's way of saying that he was upset that one so young as you should be in the battle and that his heart—and he has a large one—was grieved at the risks you were running."

I said, "Oh."

Then He asked me many questions about my life at Michael's. I felt that He knew the answers as well as I did. At the end, He took my hand as I stood in front of Him.

"Soon," He said, "I will ask you to come here and to be closer to me. Later, when I think you are well prepared, I shall give you important duties and so you will help me more directly."

I thanked Him but did not ask what those duties would be, but He went on:

"You wonder what you will do for me. I shall not say until I think you are ready for the tasks which I shall give you."

I said that I understood and He said that I could sit on the arbor step, if I wished to be in the sun. So I did and——"

"Chamiel?"

"Yes?"

"What duties did you have to do?" David asked.

"Before I was given the simplest of them, I spent many seasons at the Great Court learning and learning. Then, when I was considered well skilled, I was sent with messages——" Chamiel smiled to himself "——important messages, those which need persuasion in their delivery."

"Where did you take them?"

"At first only about the Kingdom. Later to the earth

74

and elsewhere and once to Zareal—that is a story of its own. And I was sent not only with messages. I went often to those in difficulty, who might be righted by clear and loving argument."

"A conscience?"

"No. Not a conscience." Chamiel laughed. "Perhaps a stimulator of consciences. But all that was much later and is only partly concerned with my present story."

He paused, as though collecting his thoughts, and then went on:

'I remember how I sat on the warm stones and the scent of ripening apples was in the air and Michael and the Lord talked together. At the start, I did not pay much attention to their words. I was thinking of what He had said to me and then I wondered what He would say to Abdiel and if Abdiel would stay on at the Great Court and, if he did, how much I would miss him. I looked down the path in front of us and through the archway. I glimpsed more trees in another walled garden and I wondered what it was like. At that moment He said:

"Chamiel?"

I turned my head to Him.

"You may go down there. Bring back some of the greengages which are at the far end."

I ran down the path and through the archway and found myself in a similar garden, where, instead of apples and pears, there were trees of apricots, plums, peaches, nectarines and greengages. I found the greengages, picked a blouseful and went back.

I gave the fruit to the Lord and He took them from me, putting them beside Him on the seat. He was talking so earnestly that I wondered if He knew that I had brought them. I sat down on the step again, closed my eyes and felt the sun hot on my eyelids.

I heard Michael ask:

"Am I to go to them?"

"I think you will have to later on—I have told you the words I wish you to give them. I think that they will not listen in any other way and so you will tell them what I wish them to know and what I wish for them. So much and no more will I do. Zareal strikes at me through the earth." He stopped and there was a long silence. The only sound was that of a bee searching from flower to flower of the gloriosas which climbed the arbor. At last, He went on:

"They are restless and ever will be. Thrusting into new knowledge, and the more they find the greater will be their wish to find. They will be consumed by their need to have understanding and dominion in all material things. They will be proud in achievement. They will know so much, so quickly. But they will forget that with every gain they will lose some part of those things which they already have. Each generation will think itself better and more fortunate than the last, and they will become like a clod of earth which the frost and the sun crack open and there is no center left. Only in one thing they will not go forward—their knowledge of me."

He sighed and continued:

"I made them. I put them on earth and, if they do not listen to my words, they must go their own way. I am not concerned with their bodies, but only with their souls, which are the true knowledge. Zareal will corrupt their souls through their bodies. But I will put the knowledge of goodness into every man—not according to the sects of men but according to me—and it will differ from people to people over the face of the earth. When I have done that, then they must live by their own strength or weakness. I am their Father and I give them this knowledge so that they shall know good from evil and me and my people from Zareal and his. Many will neglect this knowledge. It will be overlaid, choked, neglected, explained away. Men will say that I punish them, but it is they who punish themselves by forgetting my knowledge and by misusing it."

I think that Michael turned to ask a question, but He did not notice and went on:

"To me they will attribute all power and all wisdom because they are children and without such a God they would be lost and comfortless. They will pray to me for peace and make wars. They will pray for strength in the justice of their causes. They will pray for victory over their praying-for-victory enemies and will ask me to guide and lead them; to reveal my will to them; for power to love their enemies; for prosperity, happiness, safety. They will ask that winds shall blow and winds shall stop blowing; for rain; for sun; for the down-trodden, the poor, the sick and the aged. Yet, in all of them they are their own masters—if they use my knowledge. And, though they ask all these of me, they will not receive them, for they must prove themselves and will receive them only by the use of my knowledge and will create by its use their own strength. When they have learned and done this they will live in peace and happiness. I am their Father and I wish these things for them, but only they can make them so."

Then He said to me:

"Do you understand this, Chamiel?"

I got up and stood in front of Him and answered:

"Yes. For they are simple and clear."

"In truth, I think you do. You are right. These things are simple and clear. Soon you will remind men of that, for they will make them difficult and split them into a thousand purposeless meanings." He smiled and He was looking into the distance and I knew that He spoke to Michael as well as to me.

"Man can be content—as we are here—if he will listen and do my will. If he does not, then Zareal wins him and man will suffer on earth. Some will suffer until they find my knowledge. Others will stay bound to Zareal all their lives through until, in their last enlightenment, their agony will surpass all others. But in the end they will all return to me here, for they are mine and I am their Father."

When He ended there was a great silence of thought and I wondered if I would be strong enough to serve the Lord as He wished and He said to me:

"You will," and I looked into His eyes and said nothing.

Gabriel came to us and I turned at the sound of his soft footsteps and saw his white hair like summer snow. When he had greeted us, Michael rose, saying:

"Chamiel must go back."

So we left the arbor and passed slowly through the garden. I walked behind them, watching the leaf shadows move slowly down their white clothes. By the archway, the Lord turned and waited for me and when I reached Him He said:

"Farewell, Chamiel." He lifted me up and kissed my forehead, and when He had set me down He gave me this crystal circle and the golden chain.

Michael and I returned to the Great Court and found Basil waiting in the Hall. As we passed through it, I ran to the pool and looked into the clear water and Ragna came and stood beside me for an instant. We left the Great Court, and under the four cedars I said farewell to Ragna and Basil. Michael and I walked down the grassway in silence. Many of the brothers, standing outside their houses, bade me farewell and wished me a happy journey and I thanked them. At the bottom of the hill I mounted my horse which had been waiting for me in the care of a brother. Then I turned to Michael:

"Michael—can you come with me a little way?"

"Yes."

"I want to tell you something."

So he walked beside me up the opposite hill until we came to the place from which I had first seen the Great Court and we stopped and looked at it again.

"Well?" Michael asked.

"Michael—when I saw the Lord—when He talked to me, d'you know what I saw?"

"Yes. I think so. But you must tell me yourself."

"I saw myself."

Michael smiled and put his hand on my knee.

"Yes. You did. All of us see ourselves when we meet Him. We see in Him all that we should be. He is each one of us. For how else could He know us all? That is why we have no fear of Him. That is why He knows us."

"Yes," I answered and I was too full of thought to say any more. So Michael bade me send his love and greetings to Margaret and Marla and I rode away."

PART THREE

'It was past noon when I left the Great Court. By evening I had reached the fields near Corvan. I had no wish to go to Amry's house as Michael had suggested, so I skirted the town and came to the forest lands by nightfall. Then I thought that it would be too late to arrive at Margaret's house and I would sleep below the trees. While I was loosening Salix's girths, I heard a call echoing through the gloom. I stopped moving. When the cry came again I recognized my name. But I did not answer at once. Not until the voice called a third time and was nearer to me. Then I cupped my hands to my mouth and cried:

"Here."

I retightened the girths and led Salix into the ride where the sky's sullen grayness pressed upon the black tree tops. Soon I heard the slow crunch of footsteps and I called again. A moment later a figure stood by the edge of the ride. I stayed where I was until the stranger had seen me and then I approached him. I saw that he was a forester.

"Hail, Chamiel."

"Hail," I answered and waited for the next words.

"We saw you coming. We saw you from the watchtower. Karel asks that you should stay with him tonight."

"Gladly," and I told him that I had been ready to spend the night among the trees. But he did not answer and started to walk down the ride. I went beside him. After a silence broken only by the creak of branches I said:

"What is your name?"

I could not see him clearly. His bearded face melted into the darkness of the trees.

"When you have traveled about this Kingdom more often," he said at last, "you will know that no door is barred to a traveler, were he Zareal himself."

Then he asked me about my visit to the Great Court and when I had told him all that I had seen there, he said:

"Why are you alone? Where is Michael?"

"He has had to stay behind."

"Why?"

But I would not tell him and we went on in silence. Once, feigning to make some adjustment to the saddle, I stopped. He walked on and then I saw how his shoulders were hunched and bent forward and his gait was ungainly. I stood and looked up into the sullen sky and the forest was filled with whispering and I felt sad. But after I had gone on and seen the warm light from Karel's house light winking through the trees, I was heartened.

The forester had stopped. When I reached him he said:

"Wait."

I looked up at him and he came close so that I smelled the tang of his clothes and felt the warmth of his body.

"Why do you pester us?"

His words were sharp, spoken through clenched teeth, and his beard shook.

"Pester? How?"

His body began to quiver like a wind-rippled pool.

"You—Michael and all the rest of you. Vaunting yourselves before us with graciousness——" He broke off. His hand moved and clutched my hair and his strength shook me backwards and forwards and off my feet. I put my hands around his holding wrist. But with his other hand he beat them aside. I opened my eyes. His face was close to mine and I heard the hissing of his breath.

"You vain, lazy jackass——" He clutched at me with

frenzied speed. "I hate you. I hate all of you. I wish I had gone with Zareal."

At that I felt I was holding the boxwood staff once more. I hit him across the face. It was no felling punch. It was no more than the tap of a swaying twig. Yet his hand dropped to his side; his eyes opened wide so that I saw Karel's house light in their glaze. His quivering stopped and he shrank in stature. For a moment he stared through me, then turned and was caught up by the shadows.

I led Salix slowly to the stables behind the house and felt comforted when I saw lantern-light, smelled hay and heard the wisping of moved straw. I looked into a loose box where a tall, dark boy was bedding down. He turned from his work, leaned on his prong and said:

"Greetings, if you are Chamiel. Greetings even if you are not. Is there a horse with you? Bring him in. Welcome to him or her. What is its name? Where is Ollman? Ollman!" he raised his voice and shouted but had no answer. "Where is he? Have you offended him? He has delicate but coarse feelings at times. Now don't stare with vacant eyes. Bring in your pretty bag of bones. I want my food too. Ah—the sheepskin coat and golden belt——It's Chamiel and so it's Salix. Welcome. Was Ollman with you? Karel told him to guide you. My name is Stephen— Karel's ward—the best young one in the forest lands. I tell myself that because no one else does. Where is Ollman? Come on, don't stand there just looking at me."

He took the lantern from the hook, swung it up and as he did so a small puff of black smoke fled from the fretted flame. The puff rose past his head—black as his long shining hair. He came nearer. The lamplight flickered onto my face and I smelled hot tallow.

"You look worn," he said and took my horse. "What troubles you?"

"Stephen—Ollman did meet me, but he did not tell me his name and I could not see his face clearly. Has he gray eyes?"

85

"Yes."

"Is he one of Zareal's men?"

Stephen stopped unsaddling Salix. His lips were parted and he stared at me as though unable to say what he wished to say. I told him all that had happened between me and Ollman. Afterwards, Stephen was quiet. Then he put his hand on my arm and I noticed the slenderness of his fingers. He said:

"I must see him. I know where he will be. When you have finished here go in to Karel. I shall not be long."

He put his head around the door after he had gone out.

"I am surprisingly earthy when you realize that I can make words my playthings."

I stared at him and he laughed and went away.

I pushed the house door open and saw Karel sitting at the table. His back was turned to me but I could see that he was making something in wood and the blade of his crooked knife flashed as he moved it. He turned his head and his face lit with such sudden pleasure that, after my rough treatment earlier, I nearly wept. He pushed his stool aside and came towards me.

"Welcome and greetings, Chamiel." He stopped half-way between me and the table. "But—where is Ollman? Did he not meet and bring you?"

I nodded and said, "He went away as soon as we were in sight of your house light."

Karel grunted and looked puzzled. He led me to the table.

"You are tired. What has happened?"

When I was seated I smiled, saying:

"It is the excitement of my visit to the Great Court."

But he shook his head and went into the next room, returning in a moment with food and drink.

"Was Stephen, my ward, with you in the stables?"

"Yes."

"Why has he not come in? He should be here."

I did not answer but started to eat. My eyes were heavy and once, when I looked up from the table top, I caught Karel's brown eyes watching me.

"You are nearly asleep," he said. "We will talk in the morning."

I knew that he was troubled about Stephen and Ollman and I was glad not to have to tell him of my visit then. He took me to an adjoining room.

"I do not think that Stephen will wake you when he comes in." He smiled, patted my shoulder and left me.

I was awakened by the loud rumble of voices from the houseroom.

"Stephen?"

In the gray light I saw him sit up in bed.

"It's Ollman. I found him. He had gone down to the men's house. I told him that Karel was very angry with him because he had left you. I told him that I knew he had laid rough hands on you and that he should come to Karel and tell him about it. So he came. That is the power of words."

Stephen lighted the lamp. My eyes were sleepy and my head drowsy but now I saw him for the first time. In the stables I had been, perhaps, too shaken to heed him carefully. I must have stared at him now with open mouth. I know that for some while I could only think of the beauty of his face. He said:

"What are you staring at?"

His face was oval, the bones delicately moulded. His lashes were long above black, diamond-shaped eyes. He was sitting on the edge of his bed and I saw how well muscled was his slender body and again I noted the fineness of his hands, which held the lamp.

"Staring at you."

He smiled as though used to such astonishment. "I am beautiful. I have been told so until sometimes I think it a hindrance or a sin." He paused, then: "We are all of us beautiful in our ways—even Ollman—even Zareal."

He got off the bed.

"I am glad you came. I am happy here, but there are few visitors with whom I can talk. Most often they talk to me."

"How can Ollman be beautiful?" I asked.

He laughed suddenly and the lamplight wavered so that it seemed to move in spasms with his laughter.

"Perhaps he is not. Yet, for an instant I thought that the sudden outpouring of his temper might have had a fierce, wicked beauty."

"I saw none."

"No. But I see things where others cannot."

"What will be done to him?"

Stephen went to the window and held the lamp in the open air, watching the gathering moths flutter to the light.

"He will go to Burns with the new entrants," he said at last. "She will put him right. She's very good at that."

"Poor Ollman," I said and yawned. Stephen came and stood over me.

"Karel will be kind to him and so will Burns. But an offense against a traveler is grave."

I nodded and said "Yes."

We heard the murmur of words from the next room. There were long silences when I thought that Ollman had gone but then the rumbling would start again. We lay and listened with understanding and at last heard the scraping of stools, heavy footfalls, the sharp click of the latch and the slight shaking of our room door. On a sudden gust of air through the window I smelled the sweetness of pine and heard the shuffling footsteps die away. I looked at Stephen. He was staring up to the rafters. So I sat up and blew out the lamp. Before I slept, Karel came in. He held his lamp shoulder high and looked down at the sleeping Stephen. Then he came to my bed and when I looked at him he smiled and his beard held a thousand sombre colors.

Before it was time to get up, Stephen woke me by going to the window and leaning out.

"It will be fine. Will you tell me about the Great Court now? I am going there very soon. Because I make songs and tell and write stories. From a drop of water I make a raging sea. From a glimpse, I can paint a thousand ages of history. There is no word fed to my mind which I cannot make grow into something true and beautiful. I am a singer and a maker of stories. I can make my listeners believe the words which I speak and I shall go to the Great Court to learn more. All my words are true."

"True?"

"Yes. Because I make them and believe what they make. If I did not believe the things which I see in my mind, how could those that listen believe in them? So my stories are true. Now, before we are caught up by the daylight, tell me about the Great Court."

He came and sat on the side of my bed with his hands between his knees and while I told all that I had seen, heard and done he only turned his head once and that to the window and his eyes saw nothing about him. Then he dressed and went out and I heard his singing from behind the house. He was not in the stables and when I had finished there I returned to fetch my pack. Karel was in the houseroom which smelled of wood smoke. We sat at the table to eat. The work which he had been doing in the evening before was pushed to one end and lay among a pile of wood chips and sawdust.

"Chamiel—I am vexed that Ollman should have laid hands on you—that he should have abused you——" Karel broke off and put his fingers through his beard as though seeking for more words. I said:

"I hope that you will forgive him. I was shocked last night, but now I know that it was something of no importance. He was unwell."

"Yes. Unwell. He will go back to Burns and she will

89

help him. When he comes back again we shall all be glad. He is a fine craftsman."

"If Michael knew that I were here now, he would send you greetings."

Then Karel asked me about Michael and the Great Court. Sometimes, during my telling, he would suddenly smile or nod in understanding or ask some question, but for the greater time his large eyes watched me without moving. At the end he said, rising:

"It will be many ages before Zareal ceases to molest us."

"Karel—when he was driven over the Edges—where did he go?"

"I do not know. Yet he still makes war on us."

He went into the doorway through which the sunlight came, and leaned against the jamb and looked at the shadows below the trees and his shadow reached over the silvered boards and up over the table until his head rested between my hands.

"Where is Stephen?" I asked.

"He has gone down to the foresters' house."

"I shall not see him again before I go?"

"No."

"Give him my love. Perhaps Michael will ask him to come to his Court, so that he may hear his stories."

Karel laughed.

"Yes. They are beautiful stories. He sees more with his mind than all of us with our eyes."

Then I thanked Karel for his kindness and as I rode away he came to me and said:

"You are no longer a young one. You may come this way often. My house will always be waiting for you."

When I had ridden some way I heard distant singing and knew that it was Stephen's voice. I waited and then called to him. But there was no interruption in the song. I listened to the notes echoing and fading into the distance and when they were less than a sigh I rode on.

In the early forenoon I reached Margaret's house. I called to her through the open house door and then called to Marla. I stabled Salix and walked down to the nursery ground. But they were not there nor in the long, wooden shed. I went back to the house and sat on the ground by the door and I was half asleep in the warm sunlight.

The sound of distant hooves seemed only part of a dream and I paid them no attention. But when I felt the dry ground shake under my legs, I opened my eyes. Then I jumped to my feet for towards the house galloped a green-clad rider. I saw that he was a messenger and I ran to meet him.

He reined in and I put my hand on his horse's neck, brown-lined with sweat.

"Margaret and Marla are not here."

He smiled and eased his feet from the stirrups.

"My message is for Chamiel."

I shielded my eyes against the sun to look up at him and saw the glint from the silver circle in his tight, green cap.

"For me?"

"Yes."

"From whom?"

"From Michael. He wishes you to go to Og's with no delay and all speed. He will meet you there."

I stared at the deep, quick movements of his horse's flanks. Light then dark.

"Has something happened?"

"I do not know."

"I have never been to Og's. By Lilla—is it?"

"Yes. I will show you the way from here. There is a hard, cruel road over the wastelands and climbing through the high Scarflings. I have never used that way. You can go the river-way and round by Lake Vassey. It would be easier, but slower. It is the longer road."

"How much longer?"

"At best—three days longer than through the mountains."

"I will go over the Scarflings. Will you tell Michael?"

The messenger nodded and said:

"It is a wicked road."

I ran into the house, unfastening the buckle of my pouch as I ran, drew out the olivewood box and put it on Marla's platter. I fetched my horse, after I had taken food for him from Margaret's bins, and then rode away with the messenger.

At a ride bearing away from our ride, we branched from our course.

The messenger was cheerful and friendly and we talked freely until we came at last to the edge of the forests. Here the trees halted abruptly on a high ridge which overhung the moors. Beyond the gray-green stretch of moorland lay a vast arc of dull yellow waste cupped like a horseshoe in a line of distant mountains. The messenger pointed my way.

"There are the Scarflings. Do not leave the track, for if you do you will waste time in finding it again. Rest on the moor tonight because the wind will blow sand over you if you lie long in the wastelands. Will you still go this way?"

"Yes," and I thanked him for his help. Then he gave me food from his bag and wished me well, turned and rode back under the trees.

I set out into the loneliness, wishing that he or Abdiel or Stephen was with me. I wondered why Michael now wanted me to go to Og's instead of returning to my duties. I did not find any answer and put it from my mind.

I went down from the forest onto the moor where the rabbit-cropped grass was the color of bronze. Here I was wrapped around by the warm air and I wished that I was in the trees' cool shade again. I followed the dark line of the track as it writhed between hummocks of ling or skirted pans of cracked mud which, earlier in the season, must have held shallow water. At a sharp twist in the track, I was brought around almost to face my starting point. I stopped to look back at the forest. The black ranks of trees were marshaled to the edge of the ridge. Above them the day's light was paling to sundown. At that moment I thought I was once again waiting the onslaught from Zareal's black hosts.

The sun had gone but still lighted the sky when I came to a small pool from the edge of which the water had shrunk leaving a rim of greasy clay. Here, after seeing to Salix and turning him loose, I sat down to eat and rest. When I had eaten, I stood up to see the far mountains. But, beyond the moors, a dense vaporlike curtain had fallen, golden in the sunset light, slow-moving in coils and twists. I thought that this was a mist rising from the wastelands and I watched it until the last color had gone from it and then I lay down on the honey-scented grass.

I woke while it was still dark and called to Salix. When I heard him whinny I got up and waited for him to come to me. Then I went to the food bag and was about to eat when I thought that because the way ahead was unknown and desolate, it would be wiser to eat through necessity than through habit. To my rueful eyes there was little in the bag.

By the time that I had saddled up there was light enough by which to follow the track. I could see the wastelands ahead. They stretched dull and dead in the early light and disappeared into a soft blue haze. I could not see the mountains.

As I rode, the short grass gave place gradually to tufts of coarse, yellow grasses thinly clumped among the sand and shingle. Soon, even the tufts had gone as though swallowed in the skirmishing grit. Now I had left the things I knew. Ahead was the unknown and over it I could make out the faint line of the track on either side of which were rounded hills of sand and among them, at rarer and rarer intervals, grew a few tall, dust-covered plants like giant ragwort.

When sunlight came the whole of this land lighted up as though a curtain had been quickly drawn aside and the ground became dazzling white so that I had to close my eyes against the glare. Although it was still early the heat was heavy, seeming to rise from the ground as thickly as it pressed on me from above. I wondered where I would find water and how long it would take me to cross this desolation, and I was dejected because I could not see the mountains and so gain encouragement as they came nearer and nearer. While I was thinking of these things, I felt a stinging against my hands, cheeks and legs, and looked up to see the sand whirled and lifted in a thick cloud towards me. I could scarcely see the way and dismounted to walk and I bent low in the shelter of my horse. Although I kept one hand over my nose and mouth, they filled with sand and my eyes were stung and burned so that I had to stop. I fumbled for my second tunic and tied this over Salix's head, and then with the reins in one hand I crouched down with my head between my knees hoping that soon the storm would end. I felt Salix trembling and stamping nervously. I calmed him with words and wondered if it would be wiser to go back and to take the road by Lake Vassey. But I decided that, having started, I would accomplish this journey whatever its difficulties.

The wind dropped at last and the sand became still—dead—as though it had lain unmoved for long ages. I stood up and painfully wiped my eyes. Nothing moved. There was no sound and the air was as clear as a diamond so that, with joy, I saw the brown and purple mountains on either side of me and the fierce Scarflings in front and on their highest points there was snow. As soon as I remounted I saw the track had been swept away and that the hills and dunes of sand had moved, altered shape or grown. Yet, so long as I could see the Scarflings, I felt that there was no need to be anxious. I rode as fast as the soft ground and the loose shingle would let me. But we were forced to go slowly by the fiery heat as well. Each breath that I took was as though my head were pressed close to a bar of white-hot metal. For a shield I put my sheepskin coat over my head.

The silence was broken by the dry creak of the saddle and the occasional clink of Salix's feet against a pile of small stones. After a while I saw the track once again and then I knew that the storm which had passed over us had not swept across the whole of the wilderness. At noon I stopped and undid the food bag. I found it half filled with sand and I slowly drew the cords tight again and rode on. I was comforted by the thought that before long we should be at the foot of the Scarflings and would there find water. But before I had ridden more than a few paces a second storm began and we were forced to halt again. This was a more violent storm than the first and I had to keep one arm around Salix's head lest the tunic protecting his face were torn away. I pressed my head into his neck so that I could breathe something which was not sand and I found sudden solace in the strong smell of his sweat. I hoped that he found some comfort in my presence. Now the air was filled with the sound of many shuffling feet. There were strange whisperings, evil and menacing, and, at times, as though from far away, came a thin whistling which rose and fell in pitch, grew louder and louder until it pierced my ears and then died away among the whisperings. I felt the sand slowly stirring and gathering about my ankles; piling up; twisting and settling or moving away to make place for yet more sand and, always, gradually rising higher and higher up my legs. I drew my feet up and urged Salix to move. But he stood rooted and all my urgings would not move him. Then, as though it was a sudden light, I remembered how Michael had stood below the Kopal and watched the flying cones bearing down on us and I remembered his words before the battle and in that moment I knew that the storm would stop. As soon as I knew that, Salix quietened and with a great lurch, as though he were a cart-horse, moved forward so that now we both stood together on new, but still moving sand. Presently the air quietened and I saw the sun again—dim and orange-colored through the veil of dust. And as I waited the sand became still once more.

Again the track had been swept away but the Scarflings stood clear and looked down on me with scorn. I walked at Salix's head and his feet sank and dragged through the yielding sand. When we had passed out of the storm's track, I mounted wearily and with unwilling heart urged him on. For now we were worn almost to extreme by the heat, dirt and above all by thirst. I could not swallow and my throat was drier than in the wilderness. I knew that I must reach the end of the wastelands before we were overtaken by another storm because I feared that Salix would not endure again.

As we traveled, seemingly slower and slower, I felt the sweat channeling through the grime on my face and arms. Now we were pestered by darting, humming swarms of flies. They clustered on the corners of my eyes and mouth, scattering as I brushed them away but settling again even before I had dropped my hand. I wondered what moisture they could find at my eyes, mouth or any other part of my parched body. In the end, I stopped my useless efforts to keep them off and bore them even as Salix, his head bent low, seemed to endure them. Every movement was leaden and each breath a gasp and I slowly lifted my head to see that we kept to the way. My aching eyes saw a great boulder half-drowned in sand and, looking farther ahead, I saw more and more boulders and at a higher level, the smooth, shining rocks which marked the beginning of the mountains and the end of the wilderness. It was as though at one moment the Scarflings were still many hours distant and then at the next they had moved closer to us and swallowed the sand. I tried to speak to Salix to encourage him, but my throat could only make a coarse rasping. Yet he understood or saw the end of the wilderness too, for his pace lightened.

I would have stopped in the shade of the rocks, but refused the thought for fear that, in resting, I should rest too long. Moreover, the need for water was greater than that for rest and I was sure that in a little while we should find it.

And so we did.

Where the wilderness ended, a narrow, stony track twisted into the darkness between two upheaved masses of stone. Here the sudden cold made me stop and I threw off the coat from my head and took the tunic from Salix's. At this point the path began to rise steeply and I could not see the top of it. I led Salix until we reached the crest of the rise and found that the path ran level for a short distance, straight towards the Scarflings. I saw that the path, which twisted sharply across the mountainside, skirted, where an arrowhead of rock threw its shadow in a blue wedge, a small, turbulent pool into which splashed a gout of water from an opening in the rocks. Salix whinnied and we moved on quickly. But when I reached it, I stood by the pool's rim and gazed into the water as though unbelieving. After Salix had drunk, I took off my tunic and lowered myself into the pool. In spite of the coldness, I swam around and around, letting the falling water ice my head and shoulders until they pained and then I pulled myself out onto the scorched rocks.

Later, I ate, regardless of the grit which crunched at each bite. Then I lay, half sleeping, as though I had no farther to go. But at last I got up and looked over the wastelands and I saw the air shaking as it rose from the hot sands.

Our way led across the face of the mountains. Sometimes it was so narrow that there was hardly room for Salix to walk. On the outer edge the ground fell away suddenly and was grooved with deep fissures or heaped with drifts of loose, gray stones. On the inner side, the rock lifted straight upwards from the path as if sliced by a great knife. Here I was stopped by the heat which seemed to come out of the very mountainside itself. Nor was there any wind or passing breeze to bring a moment's coolness. I again put my tunic over Salix's head and the coat over mine. In this way the scorching was lessened. At the end of the track I saw how we had climbed far up the mountain and I thought that we might now be halfway to the pass. We went slowly up and it became cooler, the path smoother and, where it lay between gaunt shoulders of stone, I felt a sudden cold draft. We struggled through this corridor and came out into the sunlight. From here I saw the needle peak of the Scarflings covered with a crumpled cap of snow and, as my eyes followed its crest downwards, I saw the pass. My heart leapt and I spoke cheering words to Salix and we moved towards a mass of stones which spread across our path. When we reached it I saw that we could not cross it. Then I thought that all my journey had been in vain; that my words to Salix had been empty boastings. I could not see the wastelands because between me and them yawned a wide ravine whose far side rose in high pinnacles above us. When I thought that I must now turn back and cross the wilderness again I was filled with hot rage and I began to heave such stones as I could lift. I was determined to cross this barrier. I tore at them until my hands were cut and bled and I threw the stones into the chasm. I never heard them fall. The still, cold air below wrapped and melted them into silence. After a long time I had gained very little ground and then, in fury, I pulled at a stone with all my strength. It gave suddenly and I fell backward down the path. I clutched a jutting rock and stopped my fall. One of my legs hung over the ravine and I shut my eyes and pulled myself back onto the path. As I stood up, I saw the piled stones start to move with a loud cracking. They moved faster and faster, and then all the barrier slid with a roar and streamed across the path into the chasm. Some of the stones rolled down toward us and I sprang to Salix and held him. But he was still and patient. When the dust had blown away and hung across the ravine in little clouds, we went on and I was tired and could not be glad that our road had been cleared.

We rested many times and each time I closed my eyes. The sun had gone below the mountains and the sky above was like a ripe peach. I did not look at the Scarflings peak. I only wished to reach the pass and there find shelter to rest in. At some places, rocks had fallen on the path and in others the path was split open. At such places it seemed that I had to lift Salix over these hindrances. But when all the color had gone from the sky we came to a wide leveling in the side of the mountain and the pass was close. The air was even colder and I shivered. From time to time, gusts of cold dropped down from the snows which were near and I smelled their bitterness. Between the gusts the air was still and the silence fearful. I unsaddled Salix and gave him food and went to the edge of the shelf and looked down past the jutting rocks and past the sheer faces into the dark shadows from among which sudden flats and peaks of steely stone thrust upwards. Two eagles floated above them, one over the other, each slowly rising and falling with no wing movement. I turned away and thought of the warmth of Karel's house and of what Abdiel would be doing and why Michael had sent for me. I shrugged my shoulders at my discomforts for these had been of my own choosing.

Salix stood in the shelter of the overhanging cliff. His head was turned away from the mountain because the occasional gusts were now a continuing wind. I found it difficult to see Salix in the gloom. I was cold and the wind blew my torn and dirty tunic and it was no protection. I put on the sheepskin coat and sat against the rock wall. Then as if waiting for such a sign, Salix lay down in front of me. I saw his dark movement and heard his long grunt when he was settled.

The night was now so black that I could distinguish nothing between the peaks, farther than the ledge and the sky above it. I shivered and my mind asked for sleep but my body refused it. So I sat listening to the wind's rising speed and felt my face and legs creep with slow numbness. Small stones and dust whipped the air and when the wind became a gale the ledge was filled with its screaming. Its power never lessened to take a breath and blow again. There was no respite and the very rocks were wearing smooth under its ceaseless scouring. I would be lifted from the ledge and carried away. Presently, I moved on hands and knees towards Salix. My coat was blown over my head. I did not remove it because I was then no blinder than before. I crawled slowly and ignored the pain from my hands. When I could smell and touch Salix I lay down close to him and after a while a little warmth returned to my body. Then, at times, I drowsed, letting the gale's shrieking take me up into its sound. At times I would be wakened by a sudden movement from Salix. Later even these could not rouse me from something that was neither sleeping nor waking. And Stephen came to me, smiling and without words. He took my hand and we went up the face of the rock above the ledge. At the ridge, crested like cock's combs to the top of Scarflings, it was daylight, clear and shining, and the clouds in the arching sky were brushed into thin, upcurled vapors below the blue. We reached the peak and I looked back and into the darkness and our footprints were not on the snow. Stephen pointed and turned his pointing arm around, saying:

"There is all the Kingdom, Chamiel."

Then I saw the wide, gray seas and the mountains; the hills and the valleys; the plains and the rivers; the little streams and the forests; the woods and the tilled and fallow lands; the meadows and pastures and the cities set among them and every part of the Kingdom. I saw all this and it was under my eyes because Stephen showed it to me and when he had done this and I had seen everything in the Kingdom as one thing, then I knew that I and the Kingdom were one.

Stephen said, "Come," and he turned to me and took my two hands in his and lifted me up so that we were far above the white peak and I looked at the shadows with which the mountains caressed the wastelands. But Stephen pointed beyond the mists which ringed the Kingdom and through the white air and, far below, I saw a globe which floated in fogs.

"There is the Earth," he said. "There is the Earth which the Lord has peopled with His people, and Zareal, who was driven from this Kingdom, fell to Earth and from there he wars against the Lord and will corrupt His people."

I asked many questions which Stephen answered and I saw the Earth spinning and the slow fogs which encircled it. And from time to time I saw beams of light pierce the fog and reach towards the Kingdom.

We went down to the mountain top and Stephen gave me understanding of everything I had seen. We went over the snow and the crests of the rocks and he sang. The happy sounds echoed among the mountains and from the top of the sky and became a great volume of sound and when we were on the shelf he left me.

I got up and told Salix that we should go even though it was still the night. Because of the darkness I led him slowly up the crumbling track to the pass. I walked close to one side of the pass which was cold and every now and then I put my hand out to feel the stone side so that I should know the way. When we had gone some distance through, Salix stopped. I tried every artifice to move him but he stayed as though he were part of the mountain. So I left him and went forward with care thinking that there was something ahead which frightened him. After a few steps I saw it. The track came suddenly to an end, not against the mountain but over a black chasm. I could make out the darker edge of the path and beyond was black emptiness. My heart stopped and for a moment I could not breathe. Then I went back and took Salix by the head and turned him around. I was worried, thinking that part of the pass had been swept away and there was no way through. But, as we moved on the other side, I felt a sudden stream of colder air against my cheek. And when I turned my face into it, I saw in the darkness, between the cliff sides, a lighter pattern. I went towards it and found that the track turned into this lightness. We followed it and came to a cavern which was so dark within that I could see nothing at all. But after groping for some time I saw a circle of gray in front and knew that this was the end of the cavern. By the time we had reached it the sky had lightened enough for me to make out the road for some way ahead. But it was so steep that I thought it wiser to delay where I was until I could see more clearly. I sat with my back against the cavern wall and wondered why I had jumped from sleeping to traveling in such light. Then, like summer in winter, I remembered how Stephen had come to me and all the things he had shown me and how, as if on wings, we had gone up even above the Scarflings' highest point.

When I opened my eyes a soft pinkness had climbed up over the gray sky. So I got up and led Salix downwards to a place where the path ran straight and smooth. I looked back to the cavern's opening and, higher than this, I saw the flat sides of the pass and the chasm whose depth I could not see. I thanked Salix and patted his neck with the flat of my hand. I stopped and looked at the palms and fingers of both my hands. The wounds and the bruises had gone and the dirty skin was unbroken.

When full light came, all things stood out clearly as if washed by rain. I saw the whole length of the downward track coiling over the flanks of the mountains and I saw where it was at last swallowed by the yellow stone gorges among the foothills and, then, where it came out into the plains which leaned away to the distant horizon. There were no trees on the plains. As I watched, I saw the wind passing over the grasses and stirring them in soft, gray lines so that the plain became a great, running sea. I was encouraged by the things I saw and rode on until I came to a spring which rippled cheerfully among stones and over the track to fall into the abyss. We stopped here and drank and I was pleased by the savin and hartstongue which grew on either side of the stream for they were the first green things which I had seen for many days.

When we went on, gray clouds rolled downwards and they covered us and hid everything from view. It was cold and there were myriad beads of water on Salix's coat. My hair dripped soft moisture into my eyes and water ran down my face. My tunic was heavy with wetness and clung to me. Soon the track became slimy and for fear of his slipping I led Salix. At last, when I could see the white sun through the mists, we reached the first foothills. I felt the sun on my back and watched steam rise from Salix's coat. I was dry and warm by the time we got to the plains and there I ate the last crumbs of food which the messenger had given me. With every mouthful the gritting sand reminded me of the wastelands and I looked towards the grass with love.

Then I rode without stopping until the sun was long past its zenith. We followed a hard, brown way as straight as one of Karel's larch trees. On one side of it the yellowed grasses leaned towards me and on the other side they bent away from me so that I felt I was passing between two endless, never-breaking waves. Wherever I looked the grass reached away to the skyline and the only sound was of the wind shaking it with a hiss and all the plain was ceaselessly moving. I would watch this rippling until my eyes were blurred and my mind dulled by the monotony. Sometimes flocks of small screamers rose and, caught for an instant like leaves, twisted and turned, then swept in lilting flight across the plains.

At last we came to a place from which I saw that the ground sloped out of sight. I stopped and looked at the sun and wondered if I would reach Og's before nightfall and then if I was following a wrong way. In my mind, I saw each weary step that this journey had cost. I thought that I could have mistaken the road only in the pass and once more I asked why I had risen so full of sleep and when the night was so black. Just as I touched Salix's flanks with my legs to move him forward, three clear notes from a horn gladdened the air. I dropped the reins. My mouth was open. The notes died and I held my breath, waiting. They came again. Then I rose in the stirrups and, not knowing what I did, lifted my arms above my head and turned my face to the sky and shouted a wild shout which cracked on the high notes. I felt my call fly over the plain and in a moment it was answered. Three short, joyful notes. I patted Salix's neck and we bounded forward faster and more carefree than at any time since leaving Margaret's. The horn, as though for encouragement, was sounded again and the notes leapt into the air from below the skyline.

When I came to the lip of the plain, I saw two riders moving upwards towards me. I knew them. Even at that distance—even without sight of their clothes and faces. I knew them. They were Michael and Og.

I lifted my hand to them and raised my voice to hail them but no sound came from my throat. In that moment I thought of all the things which I would say to Michael. They poured into my mind in a happy stream. And when we met, I said not one of them.

Michael embraced me without speaking. Og, who stood as I had first seen him with legs apart and hands on his hips, the copper horn swinging slowly across his square chest, said:

"Not a suckling any longer." I watched his eyes point-

104

ing me as though I were a horse. "What a ragged, dirty sight you are. No way for a guest to arrive. We'll put that right in a couple of winks when we're back."

I rode between them and left the plains behind and came to the parkland where the grass rolled gently away for leagues and was clumped and dotted with elm and oak trees or, by the lakes and streams, with ash and alder.

Neither Michael nor Og asked me any question. They spoke across me and I listened only to the sound of their talk.

We came to Og's house of yellow stone which was bright in the evening sun. At each end of the house was a square tower with wide windows and before the house entrance were two hornbeams clipped in the shape of spearheads. We rode around the side of the house and into the stable yard. Michael and Og's horses were taken from them, but I led Salix to his box stall and while I was attending to him two girls came to the door and looked over. I only greeted them and said no more because I was tired and I heard them whispering beyond the half-open door. When I had finished, I went out into the yard and the taller of the two came to me and said:

"You are Chamiel?"

"Yes."

"We are to take you to the house and your room."

The house was cool and as I passed through the hall, I heard Og's sudden laughter from one of the rooms. I stopped but the taller girl, brushing her brown hair away from her forehead, said:

"He is with the steward."

So I went on and came to my room which was in one of the towers at the end of the house. When everything was prepared and the girls had brought fresh clothes, I thanked them and they left me. The house was still and through the open windows came the scent from evergreen oaks and the sound of an occasional wind moving their leaves and from time to time the bleating of distant sheep.

105

I looked across the lawns which went down to a small lake and a stream which fed and emptied it. There were willows growing where the stream flowed into the lake and a stone bridge above the lake's outlet. On the far side were two small hills backing the lake and the setting sun blotched them with gold.

I was a long, languid time in my washing and dressing and after, I sat by the window having no wish to do more than be still. Michael came. I got up and he told me to be seated, saying:

"We will not talk now. You will be stupid with sleep. If you wish for food it can be brought here. Og has company—Brigit and Mithandrwe and, though they wish to see you—especially Brigit——" Michael smiled, "you may not wish for such company now." He stopped, waiting for an answer.

"I will stay here and I would sleep rather than eat. But by morning I will want all the food there is and all the company."

Michael laughed and wished me good rest and then, as he went, I said without thinking:

"Michael—why did you send for me?"

He turned back to me.

"I was going to tell you tomorrow. Since you ask now and it will rest your mind to know, I will tell you. Didn't Xene say that when you came back from the Great Court you would no longer be a young one?"

"Yes."

"A visit to the Great Court doesn't change you. It can do. But not with you. Your going there marks a time when you are ready and prepared for other duties of greater importance. After you had left us, I wondered how strong you were in body and mind. Whether, having set yourself a task, you would be daunted by its difficulties. I spoke with Gabriel. After thought, he said I should send for you as I did—with urgency—and see which road you took in the press of my message. Not only that—but

106

besides—if you chose that fearful way, then how your mind and sinews withstood its terrors and trials. By this you could be judged. When Gabriel said these words, I knew which road you would take and I knew that your spirit would not be daunted. I did not say so and now I am right. We will talk more in the morning."

He laid his hand on my shoulder and said:

"You have done well."

I said, "Stephen came to me on the Scarflings and showed me the whole Kingdom from its peak and we went up even higher and saw the Earth."

"What is this?" Michael asked.

Then I told him of Stephen and all we had done and at the finish of my story he said:

"These are fine things told and shown you by a poet's mind. We will talk more in the morning for your eyes are nearly closed."

I slept until Og came. I looked through the window and the hills by the lake were still black against the first light. Og said:

"Up," and gave me food.

And when I had eaten I got up and we went through the unawakened house to the stables where our horses were ready. Og mounted and said:

"Better to go out at this time of day. Not so many about to ask me stupid questions. Best time for thinking and seeing things. Feel better?"

"Yes, thank you."

We rode from the yard and through the parklands. The trees were still and silent and the grass wet with dew. We crossed the bridge over the stream and rode to the top of one of the hills where sheep stood and stared at us and then broke and ran with hoarse bleatings, their gray bodies bounding over the dark grass. We waited here watching the sun come above the horizon and the sky was cloudless. We did not speak. From there I went with Og around all his wide lands, seeing the stubble and the half-harvested fields and the ripe corn. I saw his sheep flocks and waited while he spoke to the shepherds. I went with him through the clanking bustle of his dairies and through the sweet-smelling stables where horsemen tended the draft horses. I passed barns filled with hay or near-filled now with corn. Og talked with all the workers whom he met but he said little to me except in explanation. But when we saw his house again, he stopped and said:

"Good—isn't it?"

"Yes."

"Like it?"

"Yes." I paused and added, "I've sometimes thought I would rather——" I stopped and did not look at Og.

"Rather what?"

"I do not know."

"Rather work in a place like this? Like it better than ministering?"

"Yes. That's what I've sometimes thought."

Og laughed.

"You can come here if you wish. You're welcome any time. Glad to have you. But you won't."

"No. I'm not made for your life. I shall have other duties which will be no more important than yours and I'm fitted for them."

Og sighed loudly. "This isn't all beer and skittles. You only see it from the outside."

I nodded and we went on, but he stopped again when we were near the house.

"I want to know about your journey from Margaret's. Been patient and asked no questions. Nor has Michael. Now you'll meet Mithandrwe, the chatterbox, and Brigit and you'll have to tell us."

"I will," I answered.

He took me through the hall into a long, wide room. The floor was paved in dark red squares, smooth and worn, and the walls were of walnut wood. In the middle of the room was a round table, black and polished. Black wooden stools were padded in bright scarlet leather fastened with brass nails. On the table was set a pewter bowl and in it there were awned barley and oat heads and they gave a great light against the darkness of the table which reflected their drooping heads.

We sat at the table and the two girls who had attended me from the stables brought food. While we ate, Michael, Brigit and one whom I knew was Mithandrwe came in. I got up and we greeted each other. And Brigit said:

"I'm glad you wear that clasp."

I put my hand up to it and looked at Michael.

Mithandrwe came to me and said:

"They told me that you had been to the war and that you had smitten Zareal himself. Now they tell me that you have crossed the great wilderness and the very highest point of the Scarflings." He stopped, wiped his tongue over his thin, white lips and drummed two fingers on my shoulder. He was a small man, spare and pale and the few black hairs, rooted near the crown of his head, fell in disarray to his ears from which, I thought, they curled away in horror. For his ears were thick, pink and liplike. His eyes were bright and the color of hazelnuts. His nose was long and narrow and seemed to point downwards over his mouth to a large, bone buckle which fastened the collar of his black blouse. The buttons of this blouse were of polished horn and the wide belt of goatskin around his black, cord breeches was closed by a horn buckle in the shape of an apple. His voice was soft with flexing modulations and the sound of it was often of more beauty than the words he spoke.

"Here," I said, "was a perilous journey for someone of undaunted mind and tough sinews. But then, I did not believe them. Too often I have been but a butt for their mirth. So why should I? Do you know?" He turned his head sideways like a wary owl, yet still kept his eyes on me. "Do you know they tell me tales which, in good faith,

I believe and I repeat them only to find that they are but imaginings? So I did not believe them when they told me of your doings. Did they not say that you were but a young one? Therefore I laughed at them, yet I retold their words about you to others so that we could laugh at them." He turned and pointed a finger at Brigit and Og. The nail of his pointing finger was long, yellow and cracked. Mithandrwe smiled and closed an eye. "Now I must know whether you have done these things or not. I did expect to see someone of more hair and muscle—like my friend Gothric. Ah, what a man. But you"—he lifted his eyes to the white plaster ceiling "——a little smooth, brown skin, a lot of brown hair, brown eyes—a few thin and fragile bones—no muscles. No. No. I do not believe them, I do not. Come, you will tell us of your journey, if you made it, which I doubt. Then I shall know if I can praise you and be laughed at like a clown or if I can put an end forever to their mockery of me. Now, begin, my friend, begin."

I sat down and told them everything that had happened to me since I left the Great Court and no one moved while I spoke and when I stopped I heard an oat seed fall from the pewter bowl onto the table. Michael was smiling and he looked at Mithandrwe. But Brigit spoke first.

"So you see it is true, Mithandrwe. He has made the journey—of his own choosing."

"Ah," Mithandrwe answered with a short laugh, "I am a butt again. He has done well—but," he slapped the palm of his hand onto the table, "it is his spirit, not muscle—for he has none."

Then he asked me questions which I answered until Og said, "You have asked enough, Mithandrwe."

Michael came to me and we went out and walked beneath the trees and he told me many things.

We stayed with Og for two days and he asked again if I would work with him. On the third day we left and he rode with us to the end of the grazing lands which are by

110

Lilla. There we parted and I said that I would come to see him again.

Michael and I stopped at Lake Vassey and I looked towards the Noon Mountains thinking of the many things which had happened since I was on them. Michael said:

"There are the swans, Chamiel."

I turned to look the way he was pointing and I saw the swans but I also saw Abdiel approaching us and I left Salix and ran towards him with great joy.

Noral was waiting for us at the Helí woods and when he saw us he put his horn to his lips and wound it with beautiful notes and then rode down to meet us. So we reached Michael's Court and I was between Michael and Abdiel and Noral rode in front. The brothers were in the forecourt to welcome Michael, and Xene was at the top of the steps before the portals. When he had greeted Michael, he came to me and he was smiling. He said:

"Come with me, Chamiel."

I went with him to a part of the Court in which I had never been. There, in a white-walled corridor, he opened the door of a room.

"This is yours now," he said.

Through the window I saw the white ring-doves circling over the gardens where the leaves of the parrot trees were scarlet and yellow. And on the ceiling of my room was a roundel with a golden circle and in the circle was painted an oak tree."

PART FOUR

The sun threw latticed shadows across the gray, worn carpet. The room's paneled walls, painted once a light green, were faded and dirty and the evening's sunlight made them shine like polished eggshell.

David sat on the wide window seat, one elbow on the stone sill, his face turned towards Chamiel. Chamiel, at the far end of the seat, watched a group of undergraduates talking in the courtyard below. A third of the window was open and from time to time on the warm air the sounds of music and sudden laughter came from the river to which the courtyard's lawn sloped, the precise light and dark mowing lines making the lawn seem longer than it was.

"A year more here and then what are you going to do?"

David shrugged his shoulders.

"I still don't know. It'll depend on what sort of degree I get—but apart from that I hope to travel for a while before doing any sort of job." He paused, then: "Chamiel, have you come to see me for any particular reason?"

"Don't you go to see your relations from time to time?"

David laughed. "More often than you come to me. I wondered if there was some special reason, after this while? As there isn't, you can tell me something I've wanted to know ever since I last saw you. You said then that Zareal fell to earth from Heaven and, I suppose, lived—lives there? Is that right? Was Stephen right? If so, why did the Lord let him stay? Couldn't He have destroyed Zareal for good?"

Chamiel turned his head to look through the window before answering and David waited. At last Chamiel said: "One day when the days were shortening and the branches of the trees began to show again, Michael came to my room and told me that he was to visit Zareal. I recalled the Lord's words to him in the gardens of the Great Court. I did not ask him why, but I did ask:

"Am I to come?"

Michael nodded and was wrapped in thought until he said:

"I would rather that Gabriel were to go instead of me because he is skilled in negotiating. But he says that Zareal will have more fear of me because I defeated him. Gabriel is wise but I do not think that he is right about that."

"When do we go?"

"Soon. When Gabriel arrives here he will tell me."

But it was a long time before Gabriel came and once I asked Michael why there was so much delay.

"I think perhaps the Lord wishes to know for certain that Zareal is his eternal enemy. I have been told that the Lord has now peopled the earth. We shall go to Zareal to prevail upon him to leave them in peace."

"He won't, will he?"

"He is full of vanity."

"What then?"

But Michael only patted my shoulder and his face was stern. He looked so grave that I knew our journey would have little pleasure and possibly little satisfaction.

Gabriel came at last and Michael and I listened to his words of advice and to his instructions. Then, when they spoke of other things, I left them by the great fire which burned in Michael's room and went to find Xene. I told him that I was leaving on the next morning to visit Zareal with Michael. At that Xene got up from his chair and

116

stood in front of the window and looked down into the forecourt where the last light was dull and hazed by a thin mist. He said:

"You will meet all the power of evil and all those things which are hateful. The terrors of your journey across the wastelands and the Scarflings were of the things which you can see but those of Zareal are invisible, plausible, pliant and forked like a snake's tongue or like its poison seeping, yet unfelt. Unfelt or unknown until the whole soul is rotten with his rottenness."

We left on the next day while it was still dark and Gabriel was with us. Only Xene came to bid us farewell and a speedy return. We rode fast, passing through the Heli woods and turning away from the grazing lands to follow a desolate track over rough, bouldered country and through breaks of small trees and writhing undergrowth. Michael and Gabriel rode in front and we went in silence. By the first light we reached a wide walk and on each side of it were two rows of black pines. In the distance I saw that the grass ended at the edge of the cliffs and I thought that I would soon be overlooking the sea. Michael lifted his hand for me to come to him and, when I had done so, said:

"Go among the pines and follow the path between them until you come to the waykeeper's house. Tell him that we are here and waiting for the guides."

So I went among the pines and followed the twisting path until I came to a house which was on the very brink of the cliffs and in a clearing beyond the trees. As I came into the clearing the waykeeper came from the house.

"Is Michael with you, Chamiel? I expected you before this. The guides are ready and have been waiting since the darkest hour."

While he spoke two men came from the house. They wore loose trousers of a dark blue material which reached to their ankles and was there fastened by leather straps.

117

They had belts of a shining blue substance—as blue as a clear sky. The guides carried long, narrow lanterns of a kind which I had never seen before. I took these two strange-looking men back to Michael and then we went on foot past the waykeeper's house to the edge of the long walk. The waykeeper was waiting for us by a flight of steps. These steps led to a wide platform which was cut from the cliff face and paved in granite. Beyond the far end of this platform I could see nothing but white mist. At the foot of the steps the guides drew apart and the waykeeper lighted their lanterns. I was by Michael's side and Gabriel came to us and took our hands, gave us his love and wished us God's speed. Then Michael signed to the guides that we were ready.

We stood between them on the very lip of the sparkling granite. Below there was nothing but the mist, seething like steam from a cauldron. A guide took my hand. There was a moment of stillness. So still and awed that I could hear the soft lisping of the mists in front of us. We were poised as though to plunge into a great lake. The guide at Michael's side said, "Now."

I was gently lifted from the edge and passed out over the void. From above I heard Gabriel's voice calling to us and I heard its clear echo from the rocks around him. I lifted my head and saw him shining in the sunlight, his hand raised above his head. Then he was hidden by the mist.

We traveled faster and faster and the freedom of our speed filled me with joy. My hand was still in the guide's hand and I felt the thin vapors brushing my cheeks like soft wool. Slowly the light faded and when we had passed beyond the mists, the lanterns gleamed far ahead of us in the darkness. Michael's white clothes shone in the air and their brilliance streamed into the night above, so that the night was filled with a turbulence of moving light. I turned to speak to the guide but he smiled and put a finger to his lips for silence and pointed backward to the

118

way we had come. I looked and saw that, at each moment more distant, the night sky was a cloth of velvet blue and on the cloth were embroidered countless diamonds of all sizes and they flashed in many colors. As we sped farther and farther away, the texture of this cloth faded and I could see more and more of the diamonds stretching upward in a great arc until they were a rich diadem above the earth.

By now I did not feel the speed of our flight nor the rush of air against my body. But for the distancing sky, I seemed motionless, hanging weightless in the lanterns' wide beams. Only my spirit moved. Soon this feeling left me when we entered a thickening barrier of fog which reached out softly to encircle and hold me. But the guides did not falter and their lights clove a quick way through the bitter darkness. Past the fog, we came into clear air. I saw the darkness of the earth's round outline and felt the wind which was made by its spinning and I felt its soundless vibration against my body. Soon the earth became bigger and then its wholeness was gone and I saw its dim lands and the sheen from its seas. In many places steam and white vapors hung across the land and part of the earth was covered with white wastes as though candle wax had melted and spilled down the earth's sides. I knew that this was snow because Stephen had told me and he had said that ice, as thick as oceans, gripped and sealed much of the land. As we drew nearer, the air became pink in the light from the scarlet, rising sun and then I saw that we were coming to a part where the land stretched away endlessly and its flatness was hardly broken by a few round-topped hills or here and there by snow-covered thickets. Snow lay over all the land and it reflected the sky's pinkness. A frozen river coiled through the flats, like a sudden rent in the vast smoothness. In places, the river's surface shone where the overlying snow had been blown away and these polished patches threw up a sad, green light. At the point to which we were moving, the river was

119

split by many wedges of land and then was broken into streams which writhed between bare islets and so by a hundred different openings reached the dead, waveless sea. Above the bar, where the river water met the sea, hung a knob of gray birds, and they were the only living things to be seen.

We came down near one of the hills and the snow squeaked under my feet as I landed. Michael spoke to the guides and thanked them, saying that he would not be longer than was needed and he told them that he was to see Zareal and they nodded but gave no answer. While he spoke I watched the moisture gather on his hair and freeze into little white grains. I looked over the river and saw a black figure crossing it and when Michael had seen it too he said:

"Come."

We went to the river where the snow spilled from the banks in drifts across the frozen water. By now the early brightness had gone and somber clouds pressed towards the earth and they were so swollen that I thought they would burst and we should be blotted out under their weight. A thin wind lifted the snow and sent it in aimless capers about us.

The man's figure was near and I saw that he wore a long, gray coat which was tied by a hempen halter and the hood of the coat was drawn over his head. When he was nearer, he stopped and shouted:

"Are you for the Master?"

Michael did not answer so he repeated this question and he came closer to us and I saw that his jowls were black with unshaved hair. He said:

"I am to take you to the Master."

"Master?" Michael asked.

"The Ruler of this Kingdom."

"The Lord is Ruler here."

"Not now."

We crossed over the river and followed a way walled

120

by swept snow and at times the clouds let fall a shiver of large white flakes and we went slowly across the malign flatness. Where this corridor curved suddenly around a small rise and was joined by other and trampled tracks, stood a narrow wooden hut in the shelter of a hill. The hut's roof was covered with snow save where in places it had melted and left patches of jagged black. From a short stack at one end of the roof came thick white smoke which rose a little way and then, as though in sudden haste, turned headlong to twist to the ground. I smelled the sourness of the smoke and saw that the house door was shut and that, although the day's light was small, there was no light within the house. I thought that it might be empty but when we came to the door it was opened to us and Zareal stood on the threshold.

"Here they are," the man said as he pushed by us to enter the house first.

"Welcome, Michael."

But Zareal said nothing to me and he did not look at me.

We gave him greetings and went in. The room was dark, smoky and lighted only by a fire which burned at one end of the long room. When I went to the fire I saw that it was fed with horse droppings. In front of the fire was a rough table such as I had seen in the market at Corvan. On the table in an unglazed earthen dish stood two candles and their fat had dripped into the dish and made a frozen sea of wax.

Zareal lighted the candles and pointed to a bench against the table. I sat at Michael's right hand and was farthest from the fire. Zareal sat opposite us and his back was to the fire. The candle flames lighted the hardness of his eyes and made his face as white as swans on dark water. He sat with his hands clasped below his chin and stared at Michael and Michael looked at him. While we were silent the servant brought us food and set platters on the table. But Michael shook his head at the food and

121

spoke slowly and solemnly so that his breath did not even stir the candle flames before him.

"I have come from the Lord," and Zareal nodded. "I have come from the Lord to make plain to you what the Lord has done and what He wishes you to do. He has peopled the earth with the first of His people and they live in happiness and without the knowledge of evil——"

Michael stopped and Zareal threw back his head, saying:

"I know these things and I have seen these people."

"You have not revealed yourself to them."

"No."

"The Lord wishes that they and all who shall spring from them shall live in quiet and content."

Zareal slapped his hands against the edge of the table.

"I am glad to know the Lord's wishes. But of what importance are they to me? He threw me from my place in His Kingdom and now I am here. But here I am the Lord. I am the earth's ruler and this is my kingdom and its people shall be mine."

"But the Lord is still your Lord and He has power over you," Michael answered.

"What power? I am immortal and indestructible."

Michael turned his head and looked through the small, blurred window and did not answer at once. At last he said:

"If you leave His people in peace, the Lord will let you live here. But never as a ruler."

"And if I do not choose to do as He wishes?"

"Then the Lord will destroy His people."

And Zareal laughed and was about to speak but Michael lifted his forefinger at him.

"The Lord will destroy the people rather than they should suffer under you. If the Lord does this you will be left alone on this earth for ever and ever." Michael paused and then ended quietly, "Unless the Lord destroyed the earth as well."

Zareal was silent and stared at the nails of his fingers and the only sound was that of the snow melting from the roof and dripping, like heart beats, onto the ground. Zareal got up and walked for a long time in thought across the room and the dry, black floorboards groaned under his tread. Then he went to the door and opened it and when he did this a cloud of smoke was sucked from the fireplace and filled the room. Zareal called:

"Robert."

In a moment the servant came to the doorway.

"Yes?"

"Come in. Michael is here with a message. Listen to our words. Listen as my witness. You will remember every word which we speak and you will be my witness."

Robert nodded and came in and sat on a stool at one end of the table and he was against the light from the window. He took off his gloves and laid his hands on the table and his fingers were bent and agued like alder roots and the snow melted from his boots and made pools on the floor. When he threw back the hood from his head, I saw that the skin of his face was stretched tightly across his cheekbones and the points of them shone in the candlelight. His hair was close-cropped like a horse's mane and was neither gray nor white but the color of sluggish water.

Zareal said, when he was sitting at the table again:

"Michael—will you repeat all the words which you have said to me so that Robert may hear them?"

So Michael spoke again to Zareal and repeated everything he had said and when he ended there was silence and the tallow ran in ruts down the candles' sides. Then Zareal asked:

"So, if I do not do the Lord's wish, I shall rot here alone and in desolation for all eternity?"

"Yes."

Zareal sighed and shrugged his shoulders.

"Very well. I will do as the Lord wishes. But——" He paused, raised his eyebrows and waved his arms around the squalor of the room. "But I cannot live here like this. Surely I should have some small and simple home which will be cool in summer and warm in winter: surely I may have other humble comforts? Proper food, properly prepared, and the means to find or produce such food? More seemly clothes and all those things which are fitted to modest dignity? Have I not been punished enough? Have I not, through my own errors, lost my place in His Kingdom? Now may I not, because I agree to the Lord's conditions, at least keep a little dignity?"

He stopped and looked at Michael and smiled. One of his hands was on the table top with the palm opened and upturned. Michael answered:

"Every man should keep his dignity—whatever else he loses."

"Good. Then it is agreed." Zareal leaned backwards. "May I therefore, when the time comes, use the Lord's people to build my house and to help me to provide the simple things which I need to make my exile more bearable?"

Michael sat in thought and Robert scratched the palm of his right hand with the nails of his left hand and the dry rasping, like that of a cricket, was loud in the room. I kept my eyes on Zareal who was looking at Michael. Michael said:

"You may use such of His people as may be wanted for these things and no more. But you will leave their souls untouched."

"Souls? What are they?"

"That part of every man which belongs to the Lord."

Zareal laughed and got up from the table.

"I am concerned only with their bodies."

We left the table and crossed the room and the three of us stood in the middle of the room and our shadows mingled and wrestled on the floor. But Robert sat and stared at the wooden wall in front of him. I heard the water dripping slowly and sadly from the roof because it was evening and the thaw had finished.

Zareal said:

"I am glad, Michael, that we have agreed on these matters and that I may start to make things better here. If you come again, I shall be able to offer you worthier hospitality."

But Michael did not answer and Zareal called:

"Robert—take the Lord's envoy to the guides."

So Michael said farewell to Zareal and Zareal sent greetings to Gabriel and said:

"Bring Gabriel with you, if you come again."

"I will," Michael answered and when we had gone some way from the hut and Robert's snow-patched back was in front of us and could scarcely be seen, Michael turned and looked at me and his eyes were troubled. He said:

"I wish that Gabriel had been with us now. I have a feeling———" He stopped suddenly and we spoke no more until we had returned to the Kingdom."

When Chamiel ended his story, David looked at him without saying anything.

The light had gone from the sky. The room was dark and the courtyard still. At last David got up and, after staring into the gloom outside, said:

"Zareal didn't keep his word."

Chamiel shook his head.

"He kept his meaning of the words, but not the Lord's meaning of them. You know what happened after that because it is written down. But I will tell you about it because there are things which you cannot know and,

125

moreover, this time I was sent by Gabriel alone to earth."

"To Zareal?"

"To Eve."

PART FIVE

"On that morning I was awakened by the winds. I went to the window through which came the crystal light as if it was purged by the great white winds which were sweeping the last of the winter from the land. I watched it among the coy, leafless limes. I heard it pant through the tall elms, and wondered if Abdiel would come with me to the hills near Lake Vassey, because I had no duty. As I was thinking about these things Abdiel came into my room.

"Chamiel—Gabriel has come and is with Michael and wants you at once."

"What is it?"

He shrugged his shoulders and said, "It is grave and urgent."

So I went down to Michael's room and Gabriel was there. He paced the floor and Michael sat by the window and the light made his face white as wax. I greeted them and Michael raised his hand to me and his eyes were dark and I wondered if he knew that I was there. Gabriel stopped his pacing and stood beside Michael and I waited for him to speak. When at last he spoke, his voice was soft and the quietness of his words and their meaning filled the room and pressed down on me.

"I have come from the Great Court, Chamiel, to give you duty. You are to go at once to the earth. Before I tell you the things which you are to do and say there, I will tell you why you must go and how Zareal has deceived the Lord's people." Gabriel paused and his hands shook a little and I did not know whether this was through anger or grief. The story he told me was this:

In the days when Adam was first in Eden, he was

occupied in naming all the animals, trees and plants which are there. He was very busy and would return to Eve late in the evenings. Sometimes he took her with him. But this was not often because Adam was slow and careful and Eve was impatient when he was long in deciding on a name.

Adam told Eve that when everything had been named, they would rest and have time to enjoy the pleasures of Eden and of each other. But Eve said:

"There is no rest in a garden. The Lord has given Eden to you and into your care and it must be well dressed. So you will always be at work."

"We shall see," Adam said.

One day, when Adam had gone down to Isphon, Eve lay in the shade of a deodar and watched the large, white-faced poppies nodding above her. She said:

"Perhaps I am as beautiful as those flowers? I must ask Adam," and she closed her eyes and sighed. "I wish he was not so busy."

While she mused in this way, Zareal came and stood before her. When she saw this beautiful man, whose sleek hair shone in the sunlight; whose skin was clear and whose hands were fine and well tended; when she saw these things she thought that she was dreaming. Zareal smiled at her and said:

"Greetings, Eve."

At first, Eve would not answer for she was astonished, not only by his face but also by the strangeness of his clothes. These things she had never seen. At last she said:

"Who are you?"

"I am Zareal."

"Are you from the Lord?"

He did not answer directly, but said:

"I came from Heaven."

"You have brought a message for me?" she asked and rose from the grass and stood opposite him.

130

Zareal shook his head slowly.

"No. I have no message. I came to greet you and to pass a moment with you."

When Eve stood so near to Zareal, she smelled the smell of his body which was like citronella leaves. And she looked into his eyes and her heart stopped beating because of the things which she saw there. So she turned away and cupped one of the poppies between her hands and bent her head to it. Zareal asked:

"Where is Adam?"

"He has gone to Isphon."

"There is little company for you when he is away."

"I am content."

"If I were Adam, I would not leave one so beautiful alone for so long."

Eve looked at Zareal and asked:

"Am I beautiful?"

"As those poppies."

And Eve smiled, "I am glad. I will tell Adam."

Then Zareal pleased her with many careful words. She listened to them and they companied together and afterward she slept and he left her. When she woke, opening her brown eyes, she smiled and plaited the bronze hair around her head as Zareal had told her. She rose and went to meet Adam who was returning from Isphon and the poppies had folded their white petals over their golden anthers although the sun still shone.

When Eve reached the lake, she stopped and leaned against a twisting cypress to watch a flock of yellow-wings fly over the water. But before they had settled, she heard Adam's voice calling, "Eve." So she ran towards the sound and saw him walking with slow strides on the far side of the lake. She stopped again to watch the shadows of the birch trees playing catch-as-catch-can with him. Adam, when he saw her, waved and she ran to greet him. In one hand he carried a golden melon and on his shoulder, with an arm in Adam's long black hair, was a gray marmoset.

Eve kissed Adam and he put his arm around her and the marmoset chattered. They walked back to the cypress where Eve took the melon and broke it and Adam gathered the seeds and gave them to the graybacks by the lake's edge, and while he was doing this Eve called:

"Adam?"

"Yes?" But he did not look up from watching the birds.

"Am I different from when you left me this morning?"

Then he turned his head and looked and when he saw her he came to her slowly, smiling.

"Your hair," he said.

"Yes. You like it?"

"It is good," he answered.

"I'm glad. Zareal said that it would be better so."

"Zareal? What is that?"

"A man who came to see me today."

"A man? Where from?"

"He said he came from Heaven."

"Did he bring a message?"

"No. He said he came to greet me and to pass a moment with me."

Adam sat down and was silent and Eve put her arm around his neck and played with the lobe of his ear. He smiled without seeing her and said nothing but threw some of the melon to the marmoset.

"Adam?"

"Yes?"

He touched the softness of her hair and put his hand on her shoulder and the darkened fingers were black against her golden skin.

"Yes?"

"We companied."

"Did you? Did you say he came from Heaven?"

132

"The words he spoke were——'I came from Heaven.' "

After a moment's thought Adam said:

"Strange. The Lord told me that there was none of that in Heaven."

"But this is not Heaven."

"I know that. Yet——" Adam sighed and stopped, then after a while he added, "I don't understand."

Then they were silent again until he asked:

"What did he look like?"

Eve described him and Adam shook his head bewilderedly.

"He said that I was beautiful—as beautiful as the white poppies by the deodar."

She looked sideways at him and watched his face.

"He is right. Why do I not have time to think of such things to say to you?" and he kissed her.

It was evening. At the time when all the animals came to drink from the lake and Adam and Eve got up and walked among them and Eve talked with the birds and Adam with the lion, the buffalo and the elephant. Eve heard him laugh and she was happy.

On the next day Adam left before the sun had risen and went to that part of Eden which is by the Euphrates and, while he was there, Zareal came to him.

Adam got up from his knees and picked a lignonia leaf and with it wiped the earth from his hands. While he did this he stared at Zareal.

"I am Zareal."

"I know," Adam said slowly. "Eve has told me about you."

They were silent until Adam said:

"Do you come from Heaven?"

Zareal answered carefully:

"Once. Yes. I was in Heaven."

"Once?"

"Yes. Strangely, the Lord set His face against me and I

could no longer live in His Kingdom. So I came to earth to have peace and content."

"Are those things not in Heaven?" Adam asked.

"I could not find them there."

Then Adam said: "Yesterday you made Eve think that you had come straight from Heaven."

"Surely I could not have done that? I would not have misled her for the world."

"But you did."

"I am indeed very sorry. In truth, I have come to see you about what happened yesterday."

"What do you mean?"

"I mean—about what happened between me and Eve."

"Oh?"

"Did she not tell you about it?"

"Of course."

And Zareal was uncomfortable and spoke quickly, "I must tell you that I am sorry and that I hope that you will forgive me."

Adam stared at Zareal and then scratched his head.

"Why?" he asked at length.

"But, Adam—is Eve not your wife?"

"Of course."

Then Zareal was amazed and answered, "You are very ignorant."

"Of what?"

Zareal sighed. "Of the purpose and rights of marriage."

"You make me angry," Adam answered. "I know these things well enough. Eve is my wife and I am her husband and while she is happy, I am too."

"Listen, Adam. What you have said is right. But there are other things than your happiness. You and Eve are man and wife. You and she are one person. You belong to each other—and that is the meaning of marriage—not only mere happiness. And so it is not right that a third person should break the bond which is between you. That is wrong—wrong in the eyes of the Lord. What I did yesterday was a sin because I came between you and Eve."

"But she is happy still and therefore I am."

At that Zareal lifted his shoulders impatiently and said, "You might have been jealous of me. Perhaps, knowing no evil——" He stopped as though in thought and then, "There is another reason too."

"What?"

"Have you not thought about these things? You and Eve are not married only for your own happiness and for no other purpose, but also so that you shall beget children. For that is the purpose of marriage—that you shall have and care for your own children. Your own. And so that you know them for your own, your marriage must remain unbroken by anyone else."

He waited for an answer, but Adam remained silent, so Zareal continued:

"Now you will know why I am so grieved about the mistake I made with Eve. I had no intention—more than to say a few words to her. She is so beautiful." His voice faded into silence and on his lips was a little smile, but his eyes were like those of a fox.

"If Eve has a child it will be yours?"

Zareal lifted his hands slowly and raised his eyebrows, and Adam drew in his breath with a hiss and said:

"As soon as she told me about you, I felt that there would be trouble and sorrow. Why did you have to tell me all this? We were happy. Now you have put doubt into my mind and you have made me feel I want no more to do with Eve. Why did you come to say that you are sorry? I was content not knowing."

"I thought that it was the best thing for me to do," Zareal replied. "How was I to know that you were quite ignorant of sin? Moreover, you would have to know these

135

things sooner or later so that your children could be brought up in the right way."

Adam rubbed a hand over his cheek and passed his fingers through his hair.

"When I tell Eve these things—when I tell her what I feel—what is going to happen then?"

Zareal did not answer and Adam turned violently to him.

"The best thing that you can do, Zareal, is to get out of here as quick as a snake before I lose my temper. And don't ever come back again."

"Very well. If you feel that is the best thing, I will go. But you will remember that I came to you to make amends and to put things right."

"Put things right? Put things wrong. So wrong, so confused that they will never be right again."

Adam glared at Zareal then he turned away and called to the gray marmoset. He waited but there was no sign of him. Adam sadly shook his head and, muttering to himself, walked away.

He found Eve by the cypress which twisted over the lakeside. The marmoset was with her.

"What has happened?" Eve asked.

"Why?"

"The marmoset came back to me, chattering and frightened."

"Zareal came to see me."

"Zareal? Why should that trouble the marmoset?"

"Zareal is not what you thought. He may once have been in Heaven, but he said that the Lord set His face against him and he had to leave. I think that the Lord threw him from Heaven as I would throw him from Eden. He is too beautiful, savory and full of fair speech to be trusted."

"What did he say?"

Adam sat down by Eve.

"Everything is confused."

"How? In what way?"

"He came to me and said that he was grieved about the happening between you and him. He said that it was very wrong and a sin."

"Sin?"

Adam told Eve all the words which he and Zareal had spoken. But he said nothing of his own turbulent feelings. When he finished talking, Eve got up and went to the edge of the lake. She spoke without turning around.

"What you have said means that I have sinned?"

"Yes. According to Zareal. Sinned in the eyes of the Lord."

"What do you feel?"

"I was content. Until he showed me how it was wrong. Our children should be our own. I had not thought of that—why should I? But when I did, I saw the purpose of marriage. Then I suddenly felt——"

Eve turned and waited for his next words. But he was silent and sat with his head cupped in his hands and his elbows resting on his knees. She came to him and asked:

"What did you feel then?"

When Adam answered he turned his eyes from her.

"I saw that man and heard his soft, easy voice and I thought him like the flowers which twine themselves around the trees in the Seda swamps—d'you remember? Beautiful and sweet smelling, but in the end they kill the trees. And so it is with Zareal. At first, after he had told me these things I could not think at all and then I was angry and then, as well as anger, I was filled by him with the knowledge that, although I still love you, I could not touch you any more because of what he has done to you. I cannot help that feeling even though I have tried to throw it out of myself."

Eve knelt down in front of him.

"You do not love me any longer?"

"But I do. I do."

Eve wept and Adam comforted her with words and she stopped weeping and they were silent.

When evening came, they went to the lake and walked among the animals who came there to drink. But they did not talk with them.

In the morning, before Adam left, he said to Eve:

"Eve—although I love you, Zareal's words have put strange discontent into me and I cannot stay in Eden any longer. When I have finished the naming, which will be soon, I will leave Eden."

She looked up at him and said:

"By yourself?"

Adam nodded and left her and went to Gihon.

'It was then that I reached Eden,' Chamiel said. 'Eve was making a skirt from the swamp grasses. She did not see me until I stood beside her. Then she looked up and her eyes were round and frightened and her mouth was open. She said:

"Oh, no—no——" and sprang up and ran into the tall bamboos. I called to her but she would not answer. So I followed her. She ran deep among the rattling canes. I stood where I was and called to her:

"Eve—why do you run from me?"

But she still gave no answer and I asked:

"Why are you afraid?"

She answered, "Zareal came. Zareal beguiled me and has put the knowledge of evil into me and Adam. And now you come and I will not be deceived again for fear of still greater sorrow."

"I know of Zareal's visit, Eve, and I know all the words he has spoken to you and Adam. I have come from the Lord."

"How am I to know that?"

"I have come to speak to you. If you will run no further, then I will stay here and I will talk to you without seeing you."

138

"What have you to say?"

"Will you first tell me what Adam has said to you?"

I heard the bamboos rustle and I heard Eve weeping.

"He said that I had sinned although I did not know it as sin. And he has said that he loves me, but I do not believe him because he will no longer come near me."

She stopped and then her words were broken with tears.

"This morning he said that he could not stay in Eden—nor with me—and that, when he has finished the naming he will go and that will be soon. I shall go, too, because I cannot stay here without him."

"Eve?"

"Yes?"

"I am Chamiel. I have come to show you what is right. I have come with neither command nor persuasion, but only to show you what the Lord wishes so that you may know your enemy Zareal and so that you shall afterward know both good and evil. When I have told you these things I will go and it will be for you to choose how you will then walk. But for those who will live after you—your children and their children—this knowledge will be given to them from the time when they are born—as you will give it to your children. But for you and Adam, who had no knowledge of evil, I have been sent because Zareal corrupted you."

"Will you tell these things to Adam?"

"No. That is for you to do."

"But will he believe me now?"

"He will."

Then Eve came out from the bamboos and she was wearing a skirt of green grasses and her hair was braided around her head because Adam liked it so. We went back to the cypress tree and there, first, I told her the story of Zareal's revolt against the Lord and how he had been thrown from Heaven in defeat and at the end I said:

"You and Adam belong to the Lord and, because you are His, Zareal will always try to lead you into evil for revenge on the Lord. He has made you err and for all earthly errors there is payment. But if Zareal should say that the Lord is punishing you, he will lie. For you have committed an earthly sin and the earth will ask for payment—not the Lord."

"What will our punishment be?"

"That rests between you and Adam—but already there is unhappiness between you."

Eve nodded her head slowly and then asked:

"Are there sins for which we suffer besides those which are earthly?"

"Yes. You know nothing of them yet and their reward is the agony of the spirit which is a thousand times worse than any punishment by the world. That is for those who offend against the knowledge which the Lord has given them."

Then Eve asked again, "Have we to suffer more unhappiness?" And I repeated the words I had already spoken to her and I added, "I came also to tell you that the Lord will not prevent you and Adam from staying in Eden."

"We can go on living here?"

"If you wish. But it is a decision which you must make."

"Will we have our happiness back?"

"No. Not yet. The Lord would not make it so. For, though you are his children, this is your world and you make its happiness or sadness for yourselves. Only when you come to Him will He help in such things."

Then, seeing that she did not fully understand, I said:

"Because Zareal has possessed part of you, he will be in part of every child born on this earth. His habitation will be in all men. He will war against the Lord through men's bodies. But to all men the Lord will give the knowledge of good with which to fight this evil. And with it men must make their own lives and find their happiness by using it. Not calling to the Lord for help in their struggles, but reliant on their own powers. For those who cannot find profit in this fight, there will be pain and sorrow during their lives. For by as much as the knowledge of good is used, by so much will happiness come to them. But the greater their use of evil, the greater their agony until at last they die and come to the Kingdom." I ended and Eve sat in thought for a long time until she asked:

"What is death?"

I remembered how the blades of young corn had shone green in the wind-dried earth as I left the Kingdom. And I said to her: "Death is springtime—the touch which wakes——"

"In Heaven?"

"In Heaven, Eve, where all will come. There it is like this earth and its people are like those of the earth."

"Then what is the difference?"

I smiled at her.

"There is no Zareal," I said.

After a while, Eve said:

"I must tell all these things to Adam. Will he listen and believe me?"

"He will because he loved you and, in the end, you and he will find contentment."

Eve rose and I gave her the Lord's love and she smiled for the first time and left me. But I stayed in Eden because Gabriel had said that I should watch over them so that Zareal should leave them in peace until they had decided what they would do.

Eve went to meet Adam as he was returning from Gihon and he, seeing her smile at him, asked:

"Are you happy again, Eve?"

"A little. Something has happened."

Adam stopped and put his hand on her shoulder.

141

"What has happened? It cannot be more trouble. Why have you that grass around you?"

Eve blushed and did not answer and Adam said, after a little thought:

"You must make me one tomorrow. Now, tell me what has happened."

But she would not tell him until it was night. Then he lighted a fire and I watched their faces in its wavering light. At times a little wind shook the leaves of the cypress, which was below me, so that I could not then see them. But their words rose up to me in the slow, moonlit coils of the smoke. From the bank the lake water played with the firelight and rippled it into golden shreds and I carried their sorrow in my heart. I heard Eve tell how I had come to her and all the words which we had spoken together. At the end, Eve looked at Adam as though she waited for an answer but he rolled over on his back and put his arms behind his head and the firelight was on the side of his face and the rest of his face was dark. Then Eve got up and went to the edge of the lake and her shadow mingled with the fire's reflection in the water, as she stood there thinking.

In the morning Eve said:

"Adam, have you thought about Chamiel's words? We can stay here if we want to."

Adam answered:

"I have thought. But I cannot stay in Eden. I must go because I can neither stay here with you nor stay here without you."

"I have done wrong, Adam, and brought trouble to you and I am no longer happy. If you leave Eden can I not come with you? For I will not sin again."

Adam looked at her in sorrow and said:

"No. I must leave Eden which I love and you whom I love more."

She came close to him and asked him to change his mind. But he would not. Then she said:

"If the Lord says that we can stay here, why should you do otherwise?"

She was angry and Adam answered:

"I do not know the answer to your question, but that you have spoiled Eden and yourself."

Eve wept."

Chamiel ended and David looked at the sadness of his face.

"What happened to them after they left Eden?"

"They lived apart. Eve went to Jeddah by the Red Sea and Adam lived on Mount Fassem. But he was not happy and, after some years, he went down to Jeddah and, when he found Eve, he told her that he had made a mistake because at the time he had been confused. He said that he could no longer live without her. So, even though both of them knew who was the father of Cain, they were together and contented."